BLUNDER WOMAN

Blunder Woman

(The Misadventures of Chloe Knaggs)

A Romantic Comedy

Tanya Eby

Eby Ink LLC

Grand Rapids, Michigan

Eby Ink LLC
PO Box 68872
Grand Rapids, MI 49516

Second Edition: January 2014
ISBN-978-0-9860133-5-5
Cover design by David Kolenda

BLUNDER WOMAN

Prologue

Me, Chloe Knaggs, In a Nutshell
(But not actually IN a nutshell
Because that would be weird)

I probably would have been a lesbian if it weren't for the whole vagina thing. Not that I liked women sexually . . . although after a few gin & tonics everybody pretty much looked like my potential soul mate. No, it was more that I was sick and tired of the drama with men, or to be more exact, I was sick and tired of the drama with Matt M. Or as I call him: Mmm for short. I mean, how could I love him for nearly two years and have nothing to show for it? What was I waiting for?

He was too much work, and yet I kept working. I'd ask myself: Why were we just friends? Why hadn't things *progressed?* (And by 'progressed' I mean, why weren't we dirty dancing horizontally . . . or vertically, depending on the mood.) Why wasn't he interested in me? Was I too fat? Was there no chemistry? Did he rub his tongue over his lips because he was envisioning me naked, or did he have a popcorn kernel stuck in his teeth?

See? Exhausting.

Lesbianism seemed so much less stressful. You like me, I like you, let's move in together. But, again, the vagina thing was a bit of an issue. Maybe if it were called a yum-yum instead . . . or a chocolate covered yum-yum would be even better . . . but it wasn't. And try as I might, I wasn't. I was just a regular thirty-two year old with the mind and heart of a twenty-something woman trying to get the love of my life to love me back. Sigh sigh sigh.

I guess that's my defense for my stupid, ridiculous actions that spring and summer. I mean, I look back on it now and I can acknowledge I was out of my head. And I know that somehow my craziness transferred by osmosis to my best friend Megan and my already-crazy mom. But at the time, our actions (my actions) made so much sense.

So. Yes. I did it all for love.

You've got to cut me some slack for that. What girl hasn't been a little whacko because of love? Sure, not as whacko to end up in a Northern Michigan County jail while your traveling companions are dressed like turtles and passed out in a giant station wagon, but those are just minor details. Everybody goes a little bit crazy sometimes. And sometimes they go really *far* crazy and end up on Mackinac Island surrounded by water, horses, and marathon runners.

Or maybe it was just me.

Again, I say it wasn't entirely my fault. Really. I had a good reason, a sensible, sane reason. I did it all for Mmm.

What better excuse is there than that?

Part One

1

*Me, Chloe Knaggs, Currently with Megan
(And 'With' I Mean Sitting and Eating with
Not 'With' As In Sexually)*

Megan and I were at our favorite restaurant, Bud and Julie's Bistro aka the BJ Joint (although no one really called it that), having our morning staples: veggie hash for me, and bacon, eggs and toast for Megan. This had become our tradition. After a night out of a few too many cocktails, we'd recover in the morning together, nurse our hangovers, and analyze everything about our lives to death. And since we'd become like religious zealots hanging out there, we sometimes pitched in during the busy times to help out and make extra cash. Much needed extra cash. I'd wait tables, mixing up orders terribly, and Megan would help at the bar or in the kitchen from which heavenly scents wafted, making you pray to Jesus for a little lunch. It was a good arrangement, for all of us.

Bud and Julie's was the perfect spot, just down the block from my apartment in Heritage Hill and with food so good you'd swear the toe-curling was because of an orgasm and not just a really good scone. Speaking of which, I took a bite of an amazing cinnamon currant scone, curled my toes and said: "I'm going to give up sex."

Megan choked on her coffee. "Give it up! For what?"

"I don't know. I'm giving it up for Lent."

"Lent is in April, Chloe."

"So?"

"It's May."

"Well, I can still give it up for Lent if I want to." I was mumbling a bit, depressed by the teeny tiny scone crumbs on my plate. Maybe I could have another one. There was one just waiting for me on the red plate in the center of the table. Surely one more wouldn't do much damage. "I'm giving up sex for my very own personal Lent. Lent for the terminally late. I can do this because I'm not Catholic. I'm hardly even Christian. If they were handing out a pin, like 'I'm a Christian' pin, I'd seriously have to think about putting one on. No, I'm just going to give it up." I took a sip of my cocoa and waited for Megan to think it over. When you talk to Megan, you get a lot of awkward pauses as she cogitates. I think that comes from her job in a bankruptcy law firm. She says she has to be awfully careful that she says the right thing or she can seriously send someone into counseling.

"You're going to give up sex for what?" She said at last, and then added: "Forever?"

"No. Not forever." That sounded like a major commitment, forever. I didn't think I was ready for anything so serious. FOREVER. "Geez. Not forever. I mean, God, I hope not. No. I'm just going to give it up for . . ." I paused here. I hadn't really thought about putting a number on it. "A year."

"A year? An entire year?" Megan said loudly. Then she looked around to see if anyone was paying attention to us. No one was. They were too busy stuffing their faces and having mini-food-orgasms. "Do you know what that means?"

"It means 365 days of no sex."

"No. No!" Megan pushed her plate away from her in disgust. It wasn't the food she was disgusted with, she'd actually licked her plate clean, it was the idea of a life of no sex. "It means spending Christmas, New Years, and Valentine's Day alone or sober, or possibly both."

I hadn't considered that. Nothing was worse than a holiday by yourself, sexless, watching Comedy Central and laughing out loud. I've been there. It's a sad, sad, sad world. "Well, you haven't had sex since you broke up with Eri . . ." Megan sent eye daggers across the table to me. I wasn't supposed to say his name. Eric. A perfectly nice name, but a name that could make Megan curl up like a frozen shrimp. "You haven't had sex in over a year and you're doing just fine," I said. Megan harrumphed, and gave me a gesture that somehow said, "You really believe I'm fine?" I continued. "You know, I *could* have a boyfriend. I wouldn't have to be alone. I'm not opposed to a boyfriend. I could have a boyfriend and just not have sex with him."

"You already have a boyfriend that you don't have sex with. Matt. And how long have you been in love with him?"

I didn't answer that one.

"No," Megan said gently. "I think you're doing the opposite of what you should do. For you, I do not recommend a sexless year. For you, I recommend . . . tossing Matt over, finding someone new, and having sex every single day for a year until Matt is out of your heart."

"Oh. It's that easy, huh? I should just toss the love of my life, my destiny over, and date some hapless guy. I should just date and fall in love with . . ." I looked around the restaurant and pointed at the guy by the window. "Him." He was reading a book and bobbing his head to his iPod. At least I hoped it was his iPod and that he didn't have something wrong with him.

"You'd date him and not have sex with him for an entire year?"

"Why not?" I asked. "I'm tired of sex. Sure it was fun for a while, but now it's all in and out, in and out and the whole thing is boring. Plus, I think I'm a little messed up with it emotionally. Maybe I just need some time to figure myself out without letting my hormones whack up my thinking."

"Oh, I get it," Megan said nodding. "You want to give up sex for a year because Matt isn't head over heels for you yet. I mean he's never even kissed you and you've been seeing each other for over a year."

"Almost two."

"A year and a half. You're way past the third date mark with him, slipped into Sorryville. So now, a year and a half later . . ."

"It's closer to two!"

"Whatever. You say you're officially giving up sex, then there's no more pressure for Matt to have sex with you and you can keep going out and fantasizing about him and you don't have to be depressed anymore that you're not sleeping with him because now it's your choice, and not his." She reached across the table, took a piece of scone from the center plate, the scone that I had mentally claimed as rightfully mine, and then popped *my* scone into *her* mouth! The demon. I was so breathless over what she'd just said I didn't even move.

"I did not want to play Therapist with you," I managed. Her insight hit just a little too close to Reality, and I was not into discussing Reality in the morning. Over breakfast. With a hangover.

"I wasn't playing Therapist," Megan said and then reached for the other piece of MY scone. I grabbed it before she could get to it and smiled smugly. She looked at me and blinked. "I'm not playing with you. I was telling you the truth," she continued. "We only play Therapist when your mom is with us."

"Well, anyway, you can just stop. And by stop I mean shut up," I said softly, my heart beating so hard in my chest I thought it was going to erupt Alien-style. "That's not it at all. I'm not going to have sex for a year not because of Matt. I don't care that he doesn't seem to notice me even though I've been in love with him forever. I don't care that we're not sleeping together because our relationship is better than that, stronger. I'm not giving up sex because I haven't dated anyone besides Matt in forever and I'm thirty-two and I hate him and I can't seem to get a date and I'm a complete and utter loser and my boobs are starting to droop. No. I'm not going to have sex for a year because this is about empowerment, Megan. This is about *choice*. This is about sticking it to the Man, without the, uhm, Sticking, the It, or The Man." I angrily shoved the rest of the scone in my mouth in a So There type of way. And then I choked a little bit. It was a really big piece. Like, really enormous.

Megan took one look at me, reached in her purse, and

handed me a tissue for the tears that were threatening to fall if I couldn't get it together. I swallowed the scone without tasting it, and used the tissue.

Who was I kidding?

My decision to go without sex was all about Matt. It's always been about Matt.

2

A Brief (but not brief enough) History About Matt

I met Matt at a group training camp, you know those places that companies take their awkward employees to, employees who don't get along and work better on their own. So the Company makes everyone go to a weekend long 'retreat' which is really a weekend long house-arrest without the little ankle bracelets.

I've done these things before.

You have the group leader and you're locked in a room with your 'teammates' (or office workers who usually you have nothing to say to), and then the group leader leads you in an exercise of trust . . . usually something like falling backwards from a high perch and hoping to God your coworkers catch you. It's supposed to teach you about trust and the importance of working as a team, but I don't think it translates at all. During one of these exercises, I actually spend most of the time obsessing about how much I *don't* trust my coworkers and how very little I want to fall into their arms. But I digress.

I didn't want to go to the stupid Employee Esteem Training but I had to. I'd just been hired part-time at the musical society to write grants and organize fundraisers and I had to show that I was part of the team, a real go-getter, a team *player*. (More on this musical society later. Work is important, but right now I'm talking about the love of my life.) So the team-building thing was mandatory. No go, no job, end of story. So I was very pleased to walk into the Wedgwood Center (a.k.a. The Happy Place) and see a very handsome and very male individual standing in the center of the room, arms open and smiling. Sex appeal came off of him in waves, the way the scent of Axe deodorant pours off high school boys.

I can tell you what he looks like, but it doesn't do him justice. Descriptions never do, you just end up envisioning a freakish monster with whatever hair and eye color I've described and try to think it's sexy. So instead of saying he was tall and had dirty blonde hair and a wide smile (words that don't really describe him at all), I'll say instead that he was a mixture of Jason Bateman of *Arrested Development* quirkiness, with a Harrison Ford grin, and a body (I imagine) just like an oiled-up man posing in Glamour's Hot Guy of the Month. This was Matt: sensitive, sexy, warm, sexy, open, funny, sexy, tall, ripped, sexy, and a smile that made me feel like he was looking just at me, even if he was looking at everyone the same way. And he was sexy. Did I say that? Like the kind of guy that should reproduce because, duh, that's what we're designed for, right?

I should have known I was in trouble right there. A man you're attracted to somehow makes your brain stop working. It's some kind of alien power I'm sure of it.

Attraction = instant stupidity.

And when he opened his arms and welcomed us, I was ready to do any stupid trust exercise he asked, including the high wire walk between trees, which I did, all the while screaming "I hate this! I can't do this! Let me down!!!" But I looked down at Matt, and there he was, my rock, my force, and the new obsession of my life.

Two days later, I called him at his work. I called at 6:30 on a Sunday, certain he wouldn't be there, and he wasn't, thank the Gods, so I left a truly awkward message:

Hi! Matt! This is Chloe!

My voice was so tight and peppy it sounded like I was on helium.

> *Oh. Chloe from that group you just had, you know, Mozart fundraiser go-go-go! I was the one with the curly shortish reddish hair, the one who talked a lot, the one who screamed "FOR GODDSAKES GET ME OUT OF THIS TREE!!!" Yeah. So I was wondering if you'd like to go out for coffee with me? Scratch that. I don't drink coffee, but maybe you do. You could get coffee and I could get something else. Tea maybe. Probably hot chocolate. Or maybe just water. And a scone. I like scones. Do you like scones? Yeah. So. I'd like to meet you. For an un-coffee. Okey-dokey? Okay.*

Not only had I actually said 'Okey-dokey', I also hung up without leaving my number. I had to call back and leave another message that I knew he'd get before the previous message so I basically had to repeat the entire thing. It was terrible.

He called me Monday morning.

We had un-coffee on Tuesday. Followed by un-lunch (I

was too nervous to eat) and an un-walk (we sat on a park bench and talked). I thought, "I've found him. He's the One," and leaned in to kiss him. He answered a call on his phone. It was his mom. At the end of our 'date' he hugged me to him, told me he loved spending time with me, that I was unlike anyone he'd ever met.

I'd been in love with him ever since.

I've loved him for two years. Two years of incredible conversations and 'un-dates'. Of having dinner together, and movies, and celebrating each other's birthday parties. Two years of meeting him for un-coffees and having un-sex (meaning elaborate sex fantasies only in my mind), of being at his beck and call. Two years of celebrating holidays not *on* the holiday, but near it. Two years of talking about our daily lives on the phone or while curled up watching a movie. And when I stop to think about it: two years of never meeting his friends, never meeting his family, and never, not ever, meeting his penis.

I loved him for two years. Two! I probably love him still. And I hate his guts for that. Really. I do.

3

The End of My Two-Year Love
Or
One Party of Potential
Followed by Heartbreak

After our breakfast, Megan dropped me off at my apartment, and I walked dejectedly up the stairs and then collapsed on the couch. What if she was right? What if I needed to give up on Matt and move on with my life? Was I just waiting for a fantasy that would never come true? Was I ruining my life by wasting all my energy and love on a man who just wanted to be friends?

I was almost to the point where I'd convinced myself it was hopeless (really!) when Mmm called. I could always tell when it was Matt on the phone, not only because of caller ID, but because I'd suddenly get that warm-throbbing-tingly thing going on that you read about in sultry romance novels. I grabbed the phone and then there he was, whispering directly into my ear and straight to my clitoris:

"Chloe, how are you doing? I've missed you!" His voice was a curious mixture of accents: Southern, Californian, and occasionally Midwestern. He'd backpacked all over the world, and picked up little accents and adventures along the way. I also imagined he'd left a string of broken hearts in every country, but he never mentioned that to me. Before I could analyze how he'd missed me, or what that might imply, he continued: "I'm throwing a party this weekend and I'd really like you to be there with me."

Oh, I thought. A party? Did Matt just invite me as his guest, as his potential-girlfriend to a party? "Really?" I said, sure that my one word was clothed in excitement.

"I'm throwing a Derby party in honor of when I was living in Kentucky." His voice was husky. Actually husky. I felt myself quiver and then . . .

Two things stopped my quivering. Two words I've never heard mentioned before in Michigan. "Derby" and "Kentucky". I had to ask. "What's a Derby party exactly?" Meaning, what time was it, what should I wear, what would everyone else be wearing, and should I expect nudity later on, either his or mine but preferably both?

"You know, the Kentucky Derby." He paused as if this explained everything. "The horse race." Oh. Okay. There was a teeny bell ringing. "Everyone drinks mint juleps." Who cared about bells? There would be drinking! "And everyone wears outrageous hats. That's a Derby Party. You'll be perfect. All my friends are coming. You've got to meet them."

You know when I mentioned that when you're attracted to someone, your brain stops working? This was one of those times. Instead of analyzing what Matt was saying to me (which as a good female I should have been doing) I simply accepted him at his word. I accepted without question, the following:

a) He was having a party and he wanted me to be there with him. What was important here was that He. Wanted. Me.

b) His friends were going to be there and he wanted to introduce me to them.

c) I must be important because he wanted to show me off. I was a patient woman, and my time was coming. It was coming!

d) Everyone would be drinking mint juleps. I didn't know what those were but mint was yummy and julep sounded fun.

e) Everyone would wear outrageous hats.

I didn't have an outrageous hat, but I did own a glue gun so I could improvise. Better still, I owned a mother who was an arts and crafts genius. Surely she and Megan could come up with an outrageous hat that would be whimsical, charming and sexy all at once.

"Sure," I said. "What time should I be there?"

4

Preparing for the Party
AKA
Drinking and Using a Glue Gun

My mom and I had a long, complicated history. And not long because I was thirty-two. Long because Mom was a perpetual free spirit. Which is great if you want to go to a party . . . not so great if you needed to carpool to skating practice. She wasn't exactly reliable, but most times, that's what I loved about her. Her given name was Rose Marie, but she liked to be called "Willow". I just called her Mom. So did Megan. It just simplified things.

And being the free spirit she was, when I called her at Beacon Hills Retirement Center and said, "So there's this party . . ."

She said, "I'm on my way" followed by "Do I need vodka, the glue gun, or both?"

"Both," I said.

Ten minutes later we were curled up in front of the TV watching the melodrama "Picnic", surrounded by sparkling sequins, and sipping a cocktail made of vodka and something like Ensure.

I called Megan to try and convince her to go with us, and Mom had me put her on speaker. I never exactly asked my mom to go, but she decided she was going just the same. "Look, if you're going to meet Matt's friends, then he needs to meet yours," Mom said.

"You're not a friend though. You're family."

"Family schmamily. I'm your mother and I say what goes and I say we're friends."

Who can argue with logic like that? Mom painted a stripe of glue down the center of the hat and called out "Fringe!" like she was a surgeon asking for a scalpel.

"Fringe!" I replied, and handed it to her.

She stuck her tongue out while she attached the purple fringe and then blew on it to dry. "Of course, you're going too, Megan."

"I'm not going," Megan said defiantly. The speakerphone made her sound like she'd fit right in with a 1950's horror flick. "I've got at least another hour on Ghost Deep before I conquer the level 4 Zombie." We could hear the telltale clicking of Megan's computer game. She was absolutely obsessed with conquering that stupid game.

Mom gave Megan *The Look*. I guess since Megan didn't have much of a relationship with her parents, she wasn't familiar with The Look. The Look meant you either did what my mom said or you'd suffer days of neglect, meaning: no back rubs, no playing with your hair, and no Chex Mix. Of course, Mom gave The Look to the phone, so even though I knew Megan couldn't see her . . . I was pretty sure she could feel The Look emanating across the phone wires though.

"Of course you're coming, Meg." I said. "We're all going to a Kentucky Derby party. There will be loads of people, and you and Mom can hang out and analyze people while Matt and I . . ." I wasn't exactly sure what Matt and I were going to be doing, if anything, and what exactly I could do with him with my mom there with me. It was all starting to feel a bit Jerry Springer. "Everyone drinks mint juleps and wears outrageous hats."

Megan didn't respond. There was a fast succession of clickings, so she was either killing a lot of ghosts, or simply didn't know what to say. I've learned that with Megan, you just have to wait out her silences. As soon as it passes the unbearably awkward point, the point most people never reach, she caves in and gives you what you want.

"I don't have any hats," she said. "I think my next door neighbor has a bike helmet. Does that count?"

I held up my sombrero to the light. It sparkled like a disco globe. "It counts," I said. "Wear that. And a short skirt. Matt has *friends*." I said 'friends' with emphasis, and Megan got me. She knew what I was really saying was "Matt is hot, his friends must be hot, and he has a lot of them. A lot of hot friends, getting drunk, wearing hats."

"This is going to be sexy," I said.

Megan paused again. "I don't like it when you say that."

"Say what?"

"That something's sexy. It makes you sound weird."

"I am weird."

"Yeah, but it makes you sound like teacher-having-sex-with-high-school-student weird."

Mom nodded in silent agreement.

"Oh," I said. "It will be sweet."

"It will be sweet," Mom said. "I've had a vision, ladies. This party is going to change our lives. Every single one of us."

While it may sound dramatic here, Mom was always having visions and every vision was a portent of change. I think she said it just to get me interested in something. "This nail polish is going to change your life in a way you would never expect," is an example. Megan was used to her premonitions also.

But every once in awhile, Mom would turn out to be right.

And I had my own kind of feeling that tonight was a night it would all change.

We hung up and I left Mom to put the finishing touches on the hat. I retreated to my bedroom where I spent the rest of my evening flexing like a cat in heat and envisioning Matt's party and his hands all over me. I do not need to go into the detail of where exactly I envisioned his hands, but again, I say: all over.

And the party?

Not what I envisioned.

There were no hands on me.

And there were no hats.

5

Just Three Women, Gussied Up,
But Not in a 'Sex In The City' Kind of Way

Megan called her blue Volvo station wagon The Beast. And it was too. It snarled and growled and spit red fire from its anus . . . er . . . exhaust. It was born sometime around the 70's (like us) and (unlike us) it was old beyond its years. Mom and I heard it coming five minutes before Megan actually pulled into the driveway.

As soon as we heard The Beast sputtering, Mom went into overdrive trying to shoo me out of the nest. "Let's go! Let's go! Let's go!" she cried. For a hippie chick a little past her prime, my mom sure was focused. We looked ridiculous, I'm sure. Mom wore a single peacock feather in her dark curly hair, which would have been fine if she'd dressed normal. But she was also wearing a purple sweat suit that she'd glued feathers and sequins on. When you took forty or so steps back and squinted, I swear, you could see a giant purple breast on her shirt with an incandescent nipple. She said it was just a coincidence and then winked at me.

We hustled our way down the stairs and out the door. "Don't rustle your hat too much," Mom said. "We don't want Matt to see you looking anything less than perfect. I'm very excited to meet him."

I didn't know what to respond to first. Did I say something like "How can I look anywhere near perfect when I'm wearing an electrified sombrero?" or did I respond to my mother wanting to meet Matt. Of course she'd been wanting to meet him for years. I kept the two of them away from each other because I didn't want her to get hopes up for grandbaby-hippie-offspring. But the way he'd asked me to come to the party, something inside me was shifting and I was starting to believe, to actually hope, that the thing I most wanted was about to happen: Matt was going to admit he loved me back.

Megan didn't get out of the car. She just stared fiercely ahead, and I couldn't blame her. She was wearing a bicycle helmet with Thomas the Tank Engine plastered on the side, and her hair puffed out between the little air vents. To make matters worse, she was wearing goggles. Actual goggles. "Well, Megan, don't you look . . ." Mom searched the air for the word and then plucked it from the word-tree: "*Swimmingliscious* tonight." She finished and smiled.

Megan responded with a middle finger gesture that I'm sure she intended to mean: Please get in the back. I can't wait to go to Matt's party wearing this fantastic helmet!

And then we were off.

I wish we'd *stayed* off.

Hindsight, though, right? It will kill you every time.

6

How We Make Our Entrance

Megan pulled The Beast onto the lawn, slammed it into park and immediately took off her bike helmet. Her hair stayed in funny puffy rows, the after-image of the helmet. The goggles, for some reason, she kept on, so in her white sundress she looked like a mad scientist. She looked at me and said through steel-trap teeth, "I thought you said they'd be wearing outrageous hats! Where are the outrageous hats?"

I looked. She was right. There were about a hundred nicely dressed women on Matt's lawn, sipping cocktails, fanning themselves with their nicely painted fingertips or talking on sparkling cell phones. And the hair! Their beautiful hair! Ponytails, braids, long tresses flowing like waterfalls, sparkling, tinkling in the sunlight. And not a hat in the bunch! No flags or feathers or sequins except . . . yeah. Except for Megan's bike helmet, my mom's peacock feather and shiny breast sweatshirt, and my outrageous sombrero.

To be honest, my hat was in a country beyond

outrageous.

The sombrero lit up like an octogenarian's birthday cake.

And I had wired it to play mariachi music.

"Hey! Chloe! You made it! Is your hat on fire?" Matt said from his front step. He popped up and walked across the lawn. I adjusted my hat. With each step I took toward Matt, I felt like I was dying the slow embarrassment-death, so much so that I looped my arms around Mom and Megan for support. Or maybe it was the weight of the hat.

Two seconds later, Matt wrapped me in his arms, and pressed my nose into his armpit. Normally, I wouldn't say that sticking your nose into someone's armpit was a turn-on, but this was Matt, and he smelled divine. (I'm sure it has to do with pheromones or something.) He smelled like musky man-man. I heard my mom gasp a little. Maybe she was getting a whiff of him too. "Cool hat. You decorate it yourself?" He whispered the words into the top of my hat and I felt them penetrate my brain. Oh, how he penetrated.

My brain.

Just my brain.

Now, clearly I had two choices. I could say: "What this ol' thing?" and whip it into the trash and blend right in with everyone else *or* I could pretend I fully intended to look like an imbecile and this was just a part of my kooky style. I could do this. I could wear this hat, I thought. No one else had the balls to wear this hat, and me, well I had cajones the size of grapefruits. I had cajones so big I limped . . . well, you know what I'm trying to say here.

I pulled away from him and motioned game show girl style to my head. "It's a great hat isn't it? After all, it's the Derby!" And then I laughed nervously hehehehehe-heeheh. Terrible. Then Mom started laughing nervously and then Megan too, and the three of us were all laughing nervously, hehehehehehe-hooo-hoooohoo-hahhaha while Matt just looked at us and blinked. Somehow I managed to introduce Megan and Mom to him. Mom rushed forward, grasped his hand in both of hers and stared up into his eyes. "Tell me you're not a Taurus," she said.

"I've been called a bull on occasion," he said glibly.

"Oh, I'm sure you have," Mom smiled.

"Mom!"

"So. Okay," Matt said. "Come and meet my friends."

Megan leaned in and whispered in my ear: "I hope he has a really hot friend because I'm wearing a thong and it's going up my butt."

"It's supposed to go up your butt. That's what thongs do."

And then Matt took my hand and gave me a reassuring squeeze. "Over here," he said. As my mom, Megan and I followed Matt across the grass, I was sure the angels were singing. He was going to introduce me to his friends! The first official sign that he and I were serious, or he was serious about me. I was grinning so big I'm sure I looked like a maniac. That and I was wearing an enormous blinking sombrero. "Chloe . . ." he said grandly . . . and then added "And Ms. Knaggs, and Megan, here are some of my friends."

I gasped. I was right. Matt's friends were hot. Real hot.

Especially if you were a guy. Or a lesbian. Because all of Matt's friends were *girls*.

7

The Sad Truth
(Which I Ignored Completely,
Because Who Wants to Deal with the Truth?)

"What is this place? Where are all the men?" Megan and I clutched each other, sort of like we would if we were walking alone in the woods on a night an ax murderer was loose.

Mom said (a little too loudly), "It's like the retirement home. All chicks." There were women everywhere: standing in the grass, on the sidewalk, leaning up against Matt's car. Then I got a glimpse at his front window and there were more women inside, and silhouettes of curvy bods in the kitchen. And all of them, all of his friends, were cuter than me. I'm not saying this because I have low self-esteem. Generally, it's pretty good, but Jesus, come on, I was smart, and these women were hot.

"Gawd," Megan breathed as we passed a seven-foot Nordic model drinking an equally tall drink with sprigs of green sticking out of it.

"So I'll just give you the quick intro to my friends and

then a more personal one later," Matt said. "If that's okay with you Ms. Knaggs."

Mom laughed. "Honey, if you're going to get personal with my daughter than you really aught to call me Frenchie. All my friends call me Frenchie."

"Mom, no one calls you Frenchie," I said.

"Shhhhh," she said and nudged me. "It's better than Ms. Knaggs. I didn't even realize he was talking to me at first, and, Chloe dear, he is a beautiful man. I hope you've slept with him because if not, what a waste."

He pointed to the blond, either oblivious to what my mom was saying or pretending not to hear: "That's Ingrid. We've been friends since we were kids, and over there is Keeley . . ." We all turned to see who he was pointing at. Keeley was a 1950's style vixen, with bobbed brown hair and spicy red lips wearing a red dress straight out of Marilyn Monroe's closet.

She nodded. Then Matt started pointing to women indiscriminately and telling me their names: Tracey, Vikki, Sarah, Marie, Cristina, all of them beautiful, all talking together. And I noticed that they are all really well put together, sort of like each one prepped the way you prep before going on a date. I leaned in and whispered to Megan and my mom: "It's like a Wax Museum of The Beauty Queens in here." They nodded.

He showed us his house: the two bedrooms, the office, and the wood floors in the dining room. All of it nice, but definitely bachelor. Nothing matched. I felt the Domestic in me rising envisioning the colors I'd paint the place. I'd choose colors that sound like food: Butter in the kitchen, Café Au Lait in the living room, and the bedroom? Chocolate, definitely, Chocolate.

"And that's it," Matt said. "That's the tour. Any questions?"

Before I could stop her, Megan raised her pointer finger. "Just one. Why aren't there any men here? Why are all your friends . . . chicks?"

Matt smiled. God, what a smile. A smile that made you forget everything, even things that were incredibly disturbing like, i.e., this party. "Yeah. I've just always gotten along better with women. You guys are a lot more fun to hang around with." The doorbell rang, and Matt turned. "There are mint juleps in the kitchen. I made them myself this morning. And everyone brought something to eat. It's all in there too. Help yourself." He gave Megan and my mom a hug, and then leaned in to hug me too, but for a moment his lips lingered at my ear and he said, "I'll see you later, okay?"

I didn't know exactly what that was but it sounded like an invitation, a promise. "Okay," I said, nod nod nodding until he answered the door. I saw a buxom red head standing in the doorway just before I turned to Megan.

"You do realize we've entered the vortex of evil," she said.

"Oh, it's not that bad. Do you want to know what he just whispered to me?"

"It better be good because I'm wearing a thong for you."

"You're not wearing it for me, you're wearing it for his friends, remember?"

Megan and Mom got our drinks and I watched Matt from a distance: how he said hello to everyone, how he hugged and laughed, how he lead the buxom redhead into the kitchen and told her exactly what he just told me, that he'd see her later. And still, I was stupid enough to believe that to him, I was special.

I'm not like everyone else here, no. I'm the only one in the world to him.

Tell me, why . . . why do we convince ourselves to not see what is right in front of us? And more specifically, why was I letting myself be so dumb? I should've turned my back and walked out. I should have walked away from Matt entirely.

But I ask you, once a chocolate truffle is set in front of you, isn't there a part of you that just wants a nibble? Just a nibble? I wanted my fucking nibble!

So. Yes. I blame hormones entirely. I wanted to be the only one for Matt, and so that night I was . . . even if I wasn't.

7.5

A Brief Interlude

Surely at this point, you realize that things are not going to get better for me. And you're right. And you're probably wondering how could a fairly attractive, probably smart woman be so stupid? Clearly, if she'd been seeing this guy for two years and they'd never even kissed, surely he wasn't interested. That just doesn't happen. Not in our culture. In our culture, you know a guy for a couple of hours and after the second drink you sleep with him. You don't wait two years of unrequited . . . well . . . humping and think the guy has a thing for you.

Yes you do!!!

Yes I did!!! And I was perfectly sane to think so. See, Matt and I had had this heart to heart conversation when we first had our un-coffee, and it was what I was shaping my whole relationship with him on. Here it is, and I submit a word-for-word transcription of that very conversation. (I don't, really, I'm going on memory, but it sounds so much more convincing if I say I have it recorded.)

MATT: So, Chloe, if you don't mind me asking, are you

seeing anyone right now?

CHLOE: Do I mind? Ha! (Nervous laugh/snort/burp thing.) No. I don't mind at all. I'm not. Currently. Seeing anyone. Are you?

MATT: (a little sadly) No. I'm not.

(long pause)

CHLOE: Okay. Good.

MATT: I just, I'm not sure . . .

CHLOE: Yeah?

MATT: I'm not sure if I'm up for it.

CHLOE: Up for what? Dating?

MATT: Dating. Fucking just to fuck. I want . . . jeez . . . I'm almost thirty-five and you know what I want?

CHLOE: What?

MATT: I want something slow. Something old-fashioned. Something that's real. I'm just sick of all the . . .

CHLOE: Fucking just to fuck? Me too. I don't want to fuck just to fuck anymore. I mean, fuck.

MATT: No. God! I don't do that. I've never done that.

CHLOE: God, me either. Terrible. Terrible thing to do.

MATT: I just want . . . well . . .

CHLOE: Something real.

MATT: Someone who knows me.

CHLOE: Yeah.

MATT: The real me.

CHLOE: Yeah.

MATT: Exactly. So. You want another hot chocolate?

See? What would you make from that conversation? I thought he wanted to get to know me, over time, slowly, like they do in Victorian novels or like in India or something. How was I supposed to know that all that time he wasn't even talking about me, he was talking about someone else, someone he'd already known for a lifetime, someone who didn't love him.

You get what I mean? He'd messed with my head. I thought we were onto something. I thought what we had was real, developing, evolving. Something that went, sadly, beyond fucking and entered into the realm of a genuine relationship.

If I were a Jedi Master, maybe then I would've picked up on the signs, but I was just a simple woman . . . and the only time I looked like Yoda was when I had a hangover or my period.

8

Just Me & The Couch Girls

"This is the worst party ever," Megan said. The three of us were squished on the center of his leather couch, squeezed between two other women dressed in provocative date-clothes. A couch was not made for five women, especially women with actual hips. We were all trying to look like we were totally comfortable. Megan was almost in my lap. "You're sitting on my lap," I told her.

"That's exactly what I mean," Megan said. "Worst party ever."

"I don't know if it's the worst party ever . . ." my mom says. "I have a vague memory of a party I went to in the seventies. We were looking for mushrooms and ended up in a cow farm and then . . . well, things get a little hazy. I'm pretty sure that's how you were conceived though, Chloe."

"Mom, too much information."

Megan squirmed. Her butt was like two sharp blades. She sighed. "How long have we been here? Four hours?"

"Twenty minutes," I sneered.

"Exactly. Like I said. Four hours."

The three of us, and the other two women, collectively sipped our mint juleps. It was delicious the way I imagined floor varnish would be delicious. "It burns," Megan said, and then took another sip.

Mom downed hers and then motioned for another. I handed her my drink silently. We waited. I tried not to notice that my hips aware smooshed intimately next to the girl on my left and that Megan was now entirely in my lap.

I'm not sure where Matt went, but we hadn't seen him since the tour and I was starting to question what, exactly, I was thinking. It was like he read my mind because just at that point, he came into the room. All five of us sat up taller on the couch and smoothed our dresses-skirts-hot pants. Mom fluffed her feather. Megan tried to adjust the thong in her pants. I quietly tilted my sombrero.

I was trying to be very mysterious and sexy, but honestly, it was very hard to be mysterious and sexy when your best friend was sitting in your lap, your mom was checking her breath to see if she smelled like booze, and you're wearing a sombrero. Matt sauntered over. "Annie, Chloe, Megan, Frenchie, Zoe . . . are you guys having a good time?" I noticed that a) Matt knew all our names; and b) he listed us in alphabetical order. The Five-headed hydra (as I am now referring to the Couch Girls) collectively nodded. "Sweet!" he said and then rubbed his hands together like he was trying to start a fire. "All right! The race is just about to start. We're all going into the TV room downstairs to watch."

Megan elbowed me a staccato message that I was sure

was Morse code for: Let's Get The Fuck Out Of Here. Stop.

"That sounds great!" Mom said. "I love a good fight."

I nodded my head. We all nodded our heads.

"Sweet!" Matt said again. All of us nodded and then tried to stand. Megan refused to move until all the other girls had left and then we followed the sea of estrogen downstairs in to the TV room.

"Chloe . . ." Megan began. She didn't need to finish her sentence. I already knew what was coming. She wanted out. And now.

"I know. I know. Take the car and drop Mom off at my place, will you? I'll get a ride home later."

"You sure you want to stay for this?" she asked. "It might not end the way you're hoping it will. I mean, and I'm trying to be gentle here, I really am, but come on. Isn't it a little weird that he's having a party, just with girls and that you're all going to watch a horse race? What's he going to do? Sit in the middle of you all why you feed him grapes, oil his shoulders, and fan him?"

Okay. She was a little pissed. And I understood. I did. And if I were thinking just with my brain, I'd know she was right. The party sucked, and Matt was patently twisted in some way I couldn't figure out. But I wasn't thinking with my brain. I was thinking with my breasts and imagining them heaving and his rough strong hands tweaking my . . .

"Are you even listening to me?" she asked.

I shook the marbles from my head. "Yes. Yes. And I know you're right. I know."

"But you're staying."

"Yes."

"Megan, dear, let's leave Chloe on her own. You can try to reason with her but after thirty-two years . . ." I gave Mom a panicked look. "After twenty-nine years, a mother knows a thing or two. Drop me off at Chloe's. I'll make a fresh batch of Chex Mix."

That did it. Megan softened. "If you change your mind and need a ride home later, give me a call. I'll leave my cell on." She kissed my cheek and I watched her and Mom waddling back to the car, with a soft feeling of loss.

Then I felt a big, strong hand warming the center of my back; hand right over my bra strap, which was (if he'd only tried to find out) a lovely lacey black. "Oh, hey, Chloe, you're not leaving are you?" He turned me to face him and I looked up at his dark brown eyes, the stubble on his cheeks, and lips that were just calling out to me to kiss them. "I was really hoping you could stay a bit later tonight," he said and then, I swear, he licked those lips.

This was what I was waiting for. Just this small acknowledgment. "Of course I'm staying." I took one last look at the women around me, and tried not to be too obvious with my double entendre: "Bring on the horses," I said.

9

The Super Fast, Super Exciting Derby Extravaganza!!!

Matt's basement was packed with smooth legs, thin arms, big breasts, and amidst it all, my sombrero hat bobbing along at waist-level. Why were all of Matt's girlfriends giants? (I didn't really consider that maybe I was just short. I've never thought of myself as short. Mom says I have a big personality.) Matt let go of my hand and I had the distinct feeling that the other women were watching me. I smiled, and then quickly erased the smile from my face; I didn't want to be the center of a girl-on-girl brawl should Matt leave the room to get popcorn.

"All right!" he said. "Come on everyone!" He sat on the couch in the center of the room and we all surrounded him. I looked for the fans and grapes but thankfully there weren't any: just an empty finished basement with an enormous TV and a sectional couch. It struck me that this was where Matt probably spent most of his time: alone, watching TV on his gigantic couch. It was sad. "It should be on any second here," he said excitedly. I looked around to see if any one of us looked interested. No one did. One woman was fluffing her brown hair, another flipped through a sports magazine, and a third woman (who looked almost like my twin) sat on a foldout chair in the corner trying to wipe tears from her eyes.

Matt pushed the remote and his giant TV suddenly boomed to life with swelling music and close-ups of horse nostrils and women in outrageous hats. Finally! There they were! Outrageous hats! I looked around smugly but no one seemed to notice.

Then the race was on. Matt leaned forward and all the women followed. "Come on come on come on!" he said. A sporty type woman sat next to him and they both said: "Come on you bastard, run!"

And then it was over.

"Wow! That was amazing!" Matt said and wiped the sweat from his forehead.

I looked at my watch and before I could stop myself, words were pouring out of my mouth. "That's it? That's the race?"

Matt looked at me as if seeing me for the first time. "Yep. That's the race. Why? What's wrong? You didn't like it?"

I swallowed. The crying girl in the corner nodded as if to encourage me. "Well, I mean, this whole party, this build up, all this foreplay and it lasts two minutes?"

It was like the room collectively gasped.

Matt smiled. "Was it as good for you as it was for me?"

10

Oh, Rhett!

"Whatever," I said. I lifted my chin into the air and I sincerely hoped there was a spotlight on my sombrero because this *was* the dumbest party ever. I mean, a party with all the women drinking bad drinks and pretending to have a good time just to be close to one guy? And then the horse race that everyone was so pumped up about lasted two minutes, tops. Two minutes! I couldn't even *say* the word 'orgasm' (let alone have an orgasm) in the length of the time it took those horses to run around a circle.

On that note, I huffed, spun around and marched out of the basement.

It wasn't just the stupid party I was mad about. I was mad at Matt. I honestly thought, I believed that there was something between us, affection, lust, love, something, and that whatever had been holding him back had disintegrated . . . the way a cheap, cute skirt from H&M disintegrates if you wash it. I had convinced myself that something that clearly wasn't there, was there, and I'd had enough. It was time to walk away from the party, from Matt, and from the stupid fantasy world I was living in. Matt did not love me. I'd been wasting all my time and energy and on man I didn't even know.

Me and my hat pushed our way through breasts lifted skyward by too tight dresses and the smooth arms and perfumed necks, then up the stairs clomp clomp clomp (take that, Derby) and through the living room, and out the door and . . .

"Chloe! Wait!" It was him. Good God. He'd run after me. I didn't think he'd follow. Honestly. I mean usually, when I make a scene or something it's for exactly that sort of thing: to get a guy to follow/love/chase me. But this time I just wanted out. I stopped dead in my tracks, which really was stopping in my tracks. I'd walked into the center of his lawn and it was all squishy from too much watering. In fact, I think I was sinking. My heart hammered a drum solo. A really long drum solo, because suddenly Matt's hot hand was on my shoulder. "Hey," he said softly and then took my hat gently off my head, and tossed it on the grass. I turned to look up at him. "Don't you want to know who won?"

He'd asked me a question and all I could do was look at those lips. Those perfect, manly, soft, yummy lips . . . and he wanted to know if I cared about who won? They were horses! Running in a circle! Did I care who won? "No," I said.

"Oh," he said, and then his hand tilted my head a little. "Because you did." And then he kissed me.

Sweet Buddha, angels singing, Matt M, or Mmmmmm, kissed me.

In front of a hundred pairs of mascaraed eyes.

11

A Choice Between a Rock and a Hard Place.
Mmmmm's Hard Place.

When Matt kissed me, it was like . . . wow. How do I explain this? Imagine fans blowing and someone spritzing his muscles with oil, and me clasping a sheet to my burgeoning bosoms, and Barry White is playing in the background singing something like "Ooooh, baby, take those panties off . . ."

Naaaah. I'm just joking. It wasn't like that at all. But it *was* hot. He leaned in and I stood on my tippy toes, he tilted my head back with his big hands, and then his lips were on me: firm, strong, wet. Just a little pressure at first and then the hint of a tongue, and then, (dear God I do believe in you!) choirs were singing and pulsing and jumping and . . . oops . . . not a choir, that was my clitoris. Easy to get that confused sometimes.

God.

It was good.

He was good.

He kissed me so long and deep and unhurried, that I

felt it in my toes. It was a kiss full of promise of what's to come, and I mean, come, yes *that* kind, of promised pleasures, but it seemed to hint at something else. It seemed to promise . . . I don't know . . . a future.

We pulled apart. I looked at him. He looked at me. "Wow," we said. "Wow."

And then my phone rang.

And rang.

"You going to answer that?" Matt asked, a little hint of a smile still lingering on his lips. (Those lips! Those lips I had just kissed!)

"No," I said. The phone rang. "If you could just, you know, kiss me one more time, maybe it will stop." He pulled me to him, I lifted my chin, and the stupid phone rang again. "Shit shit shit," I murmured and flicked it open. "Hello!" I said, and yes, there was agitation in my voice.

"Chloe?" Mom said my name and it was all I need to hear that something was wrong. Really wrong.

"What's wrong? Are you okay? Where are you? Where's Megan?" I stepped away from Matt. For a moment I forgot about his hot lips and the possibility of getting naked with him at long last. I was just thinking about Megan as I listened to my mom cry.

"Aw, shit, Chloe," she managed after a moment. "That fucking chipmunk. I saw a fucking chipmunk and grabbed the steering wheel from Megan and . . ."

"And? Are you okay? Is Megan okay?" My heart was pounding harder this time and I didn't care anymore about Matt or kissing or whatever.

Mom breathed. "Oh, sure. I'm okay. Just freaked out. Megan's mostly okay. It's just, I sort of got us into a car accident."

"What? WHAT? What does 'mostly okay' mean exactly? Megan isn't dead or anything, right?"

"Dead? Good, God, no. She's not dead, just, well, sort of broken a little bit. Not big breaks, just her leg. And her arm. And I think she's a little pissed off at me, which I'm hoping you can smooth over. I mean when I saw that chipmunk, I just reacted, you know? How did I know there was an light pole on the side of . . ."

"Where are you?" I asked. She gave me the details. All I needed to hear was St. Mary's Hospital. I was already calling a taxi.

"I'll see you later!" I said to Matt and waved. I didn't even turn to see if he watched me leave. But I did hear something, something I didn't think too much about at the time. I heard him call my name one last time and then I'm sure I heard the words "I'm sorry".

You always have *What If's*, no matter what you do. I wonder now what if Chloe and Mom hadn't left the party, or what if they left the party just one minute later and the stupid chipmunk had already crossed the road. What if I had stayed at the party?

Yeah. That sort of thinking will make you certifiable. Seriously. The truth is, Megan and Mom did leave, and they did get in an accident and I did leave the party with Matt standing there watching me go. I left him there all hot and bothered just primed for Amber to slide in to my place, and most importantly, I did go and see Megan and St. Mary's where my mom was trying to perform Reiki on her. I went and saw her at the hospital because she was my best friend, and really, when your best friend is hurt, nothing else matters.

Not even the love of your life.

12

Details, Schmetails

"How are you doing, sunshine?" I asked Megan. She was propped up on my couch surrounded by Hollywood gossip magazines, yellow legal pads from the attorney she worked for, and empty takeout containers. She was trying to type up some Bankruptcy filings into her computer, but had grown tired of it after an hour. So, we had Deadwood playing on the DVD . . . a sure cure for when you were feeling blue. And Megan was a little blue.

If Megan had a relationship with her parents, she might have decided to recuperate with them; I'm sure she hoped for that somewhere inside her heart. Instead, very smartly I think, she decided to recover at my place instead of in her one-bedroom apartment. "What if I get a blood clot and it goes to my brain? They wouldn't find my body until my stack of *In Touch* magazines started piling up. No, Chloe, I'll be your roommate for a few days. It's safer that way."

That was two weeks ago. I didn't mind. I actually liked having her there. It was nice having someone to come home to and talk about your day with. I was actually thinking of breaking her other leg when she got the cast off just so she'd stay. Plus even with tips from waitressing and all the freelance grants I could muster, expenses were still tight. I'd blame it on the economy, but I think it had more to do with me. I was terrible with money. At any rate, "How are you doing, sunshine?" I asked.

Megan looked up at me from her magazine and scrunched her face. "Sunshine? When did you start calling me *sunshine*? You're turning weirdly motherly, Chloe. Even more motherly than your mother. You're mom just gives me a healing crystal necklace, chants a bit, and then pops open a beer. But you . . . you're starting to freak me out."

I lifted up her feet, slid underneath them on the couch and propped them on my lap. "It is weird isn't it?" I said, truly puzzled. "I like being roommates. I think it's cozy."

"I think you need to get married or at least move in with a man. Pretty soon you're going to start rubbing my back."

I scratched my nose. "Do you need a back rub?" I offered.

"No! I need you to stop catering to me and go out and *do* something. Don't you have to work or something?"

I shrugged. I had my own stack of grants to write. The trouble with being a freelancer is that it was hard to be motivated to work. Everything else in life seemed so much more interesting.

Megan continued: "I don't think it's just my leg that's making you act this way. Are you ever going to tell me what happened that night?"

I sighed. She was talking about That Night. The night she and my mom got in the stupid car accident. The night we went to the party. The night Matt, at long last, kissed me. I'd kept my kiss with Matt a secret from her because I wanted to spare her the pain of knowing she'd interrupted what would have been a fantasy-come-true: a romp with Mmmmm.

"Well," I began, drawing out the word. I was excited to finally tell her. "We kissed. I mean he kissed me, in front of everyone, well, not in front of them, in his front lawn but if they were looking out the window and had turned on a light or something I'm sure they'd have seen us. We made out for at least thirty full seconds and then . . ."

"And then what?"

"Mom called." I tried to say it gently so she wouldn't feel too bad.

"Oh, yeah! I remember. Your mom called because I was in the *hospital.*"

"Right." I paused. She wasn't offering me an apology. Why didn't she look like she felt sad? Where was my apology? "I would have kept kissing him too, probably made it to his bedroom, might have even heard him tell me he's in love with me, but Mom called. About your accident." I was trying to be gentle. Honestly.

Megan harrumphed. "Ha! I'm not apologizing for getting in a car accident. It was partly your mom's fault for freaking out over that chipmunk. She said later she was afraid it was her grandmother reincarnated. I've got a broken leg here, Chloe. This is serious."

Ah. She had me there. And as much as I felt like my heart was serious too, it wasn't exactly broken. "I'm sorry," I said. "If it weren't for me, if I hadn't dragged you and Mom to that ridiculous party, you never would've avoided my reincarnated grandma and broken your leg."

"I'm sorry too." Megan said. "If it weren't for me, maybe you and Matt would've finally done all the things you've been dreaming about."

I sighed again. Oh, how I still wanted to do things with him. But there was another reason why I was acting weird. Another reason I felt out of sorts. He'd kissed me, we'd had this moment, I rushed off to the hospital and . . ."That's not the worst part of it. The worst thing is, he hasn't called."

Megan blinked. If she were a computer, there would've been a spinning ball above her head as she processed. "Well, a) He's a guy and b) He's Matt. You should call *him*."

"I have."

"Call him again. Maybe he's busy or something."

"I have called him again. I've called him like twenty times."

"Twenty?"

"Maybe thirty, but it's been two weeks and I haven't heard a word from him! I mean, I expected him to wait three days tops, after a kiss like that, but two weeks . . . sixteen days! Maybe something's wrong with him! Maybe I should go over to his house and see if he had a stroke or something."

"You think he had a stroke?"

"Or a heart attack. Or there was that lightning storm."

"What lightening storm?" Megan asked.

"You know. That lightning storm. In Detroit. Which is only two and half hours from here so maybe there was a stray bolt or something. Maybe he was struck by a bolt and is dead in the middle of his yard, right were we kissed."

"Yeah but wasn't everybody watching?"

"Okay. Maybe he's not struck by lightning but I just have this feeling . . ."

"I hate when you have a feeling."

"I know." I flicked her feet off of me and jumped up. "You want to go to his house with me? See if he's okay?"

Megan gave me one of her long silences again. "Can your mom come?"

Mom and Megan were like best friends in the making, I swear. "Yes," I said. Anything!

Then she paused again and finally, finally said, "Okay."

13

Rock On

You could barely tell that Megan ran into that light pole. There was hardly a dent on The Beast, but there was, regrettably, a little red chipmunk-shaped smear on her front tire. I told Mom and Megan so and watched Horror spread across their faces. "Grandma!" Mom exclaimed.

"Am I a murderer if it's not a full person but a reincarnated person?" Megan asked.

"Were you guys separated at birth or something? You're freaking me out! I was just joking!"

Mom sighed. "Oh. We knew that, right Megs?"

"Right."

"I get to drive, yes?" I asked looking at Megan's leg. Driving The Beast would be a dream come true. Megan didn't answer. She was in denial I'm sure and sat sideways in the backseat with her leg propped on the seat. Her legs formed a giant upside down V.

"It's a good thing you do yoga," I said as I crawled behind the wheel.

Jesus.

Where were the foot petals on the thing? It was like reaching into the abyss with my toes. Okay. There they were.

Mom climbed into the passenger seat. She flipped open the passenger side mirror and quickly wrapped her fluffy brown hair in a flowery scarf. Then she applied magenta colored lipstick, and topped the whole look with a pair of pink sunglasses. "Haven't I always told you that wherever you go, you should make an entrance?"

Indeed.

After Megan and I both put on the magenta lipstick, I put the key in the ignition, pulled out of the driveway and gunned it.

Of course, I gunned it to the stop sign, which was only thirty feet away, but I felt setting the mood was important.

Megan handed me her iPod. "Try track 33," she said.

I pressed the magic numbers. "Welcome to the Jungle" blared. "You always pick the perfect song," I said, but Megan and my mom weren't listening. They were too busy head banging to care.

14

What a Difference a Couple of Weeks Make

We parked The Beast in front of Matt's house and sat for a few moments, quietly listening to the tick of the engine as the creature, I mean, the car took a quick nap. His house looked different than it did at the party. True, it was nearly dark when I saw him last and my perception had that "Have Sex with Me Now" sort of haze about it, but something was decidedly different. What was it? "Does this place look weird to you guys?" I asked Megan and Mom. They stared.

Megan propped herself up and leaned forward. There was a long silence before she spoke. "Yep."

"You betcha," Mom said.

"Exactly," I said. "Something is weird. But what it is?"

"It's clean," Mom offered.

Before I could dismiss it, I realized that Megan was right. The place wasn't clean, exactly, more like . . . tidy. The lawn was mowed. The tree looks trimmed. There was a welcome flag fluttering in the breeze and a vase of mums or something sitting on the front stoop. "What the fuck?" I murmured. My first thought was: Has Matt gone gay? That would explain a lot, actually. All the girlfriends, the years of no action, the sudden tiptoe into the heterosexual lake with me with a hot sloppy kiss.

Ugh. Who was I kidding? Matt? Gay? No. No way.

"Who's that?" Megan asked and pointed.

There was a woman watering the mums. She was tall. At least I thought she was tall because all I could see were her legs. Beautiful legs. Long, brown, glowy. She must wax or something. My legs could poke an eye out, they were so hairy. But this woman. God. She was wearing a short little skorty type thing in khaki and a tank top that was all silky. I hadn't even thought about dressing up to come over and see him and was still in my Sex Pistols t-shirt (from my high school wardrobe) and a pair of yoga pants that were stretched a bit past their limit. "Maybe it's his sister," I said hopefully. And then I noticed her hair: thick, lush and the color of sun tea with actual sunbeams flashing through it.

"Does Matt have a sister?" Megan asked.

"No." And then I opened the car door and got out.

"Chloe . . . I don't think this is a good idea. I'm getting a distinct vibe and aura that this is not a good idea," Mom said, but I started walking. I didn't even help Megan out, knowing maybe that this was going to be a short stay.

"Excuse me!" I called, waving my hand like a well-adjusted Mormon on a mission. "Yo hooo!!! I'm looking for Matt. Is he here?" What was really saying in women-speak was: "Who the fuck are you with your long legs and killer boobs and long hair and why are you watering his plants when he never even *had* plants two weeks ago?"

"Sure," she said and flashed me a smile. "He's in the

bedroom. I'll go wake him up. He's just exhausted from celebrating our good news," she said and this time it was her solitaire diamond ring that flashed.

15

Over. Finished. Kaput.
Or
Heartbreak, Plain, Simple, and Unglazed.

I thought: I can't breathe. I can't breathe. I am breathing, but it's not possible, because I can't breathe.

I just stood there, not breathing. I don't know for how long, but it was long enough that Mom managed to pull Megan out of the car and hobble up the driveway with her. I must have been there for ages, not breathing, not feeling, just waiting for the Watering Goddess to go inside and wake her fiancé up, and long enough for Matt to come to the door, run his hands through his just-had-sex hair and say: "Oh, hey! Chloe! I'm glad you stopped by. I've been meaning to tell you . . . I wanted to explain something . . ."

Then I breathed. "You fucking piece of shit!" I said and then I turned and ran.

It would have been very satisfying if I screamed at him, ran, and took off with a good ear-splitting peel out sound from The Beast, but I had to wait at the bottom of his driveway for about five minutes while Megan and Mom limped to catch up to me.

"Don't say anything," I said and held up my hand. "I know I must look ridiculous."

"He's the one that looks ridiculous! Maybe I can look in one of my old Wiccan books and find some kind of curse. Hairy ears, decreased sex drive something . . ."

"Forget that! Let me at him, Chloe, I'll . . ." Megan paused.

"What will you do? Slap him for me?"

"No. I'll kick him. Where it counts. With this." She pointed to her cast. We slowly made our way back to the car. Mom tried to take the keys from me, but I was being stubborn, and pissy, and wanting the control of The Beast beneath me.

Matt watched from the porch and his fiancé (his fucking fiancé!) had gone inside to do Pilates or something. Mom helped Megan in the backseat, slid in next to me, and I got behind the wheel, and silently put the car in reverse.

I made it a good block and a half before I had to pull over to the side of the road.

"Prick," Megan said.

"I'm sure I have a spell for a weak bladder somewhere," Mom said and rummaged in her bag.

And then I burst into tears.

Part Two

16

Me, Helplessly Stuck in my Brain

Three weeks later, I was still replaying the sequence of events in my head. If I somehow changed a detail, would everything end up different? No. It never did. Things remained, three weeks later, exactly as I had left them.

The summary: I met Matt, fell in love with him, finally kissed him and at the exact moment I was probably going to follow him inside for some naked bonding, I left him to go see Megan at the hospital. While I talked to Megan, Matt snuggled up with Amber. Two days later he was engaged.

It didn't make sense! What piece of logic was I missing? Where did she come from . . . besides like a Playboy magazine? Was she a love at first site type of thing . . . or was it something worse? Had he known Amber before? Had he?

I crunched the popcorn and dug my hand into the bowl Megan was holding. We were curled up on the couch, doing what had now become our pattern: watching Lord of the Rings and analyzing each other. Actually, it was more like we just analyzed me. Either Megan didn't need it or she just wasn't ready to talk about Eric.

We found comfort in Lord of the Rings. I liked it because I could drool over the lusty Hobbits (I've always had a thing for Little People), and Megan liked it because she felt she was connecting with her people. Her people being, of course, The Elves. She felt that she was an elf in a past life, and it was why the tips of her ears were ever so slightly pointed. I almost believed her. After all, she actually understood what they were saying in the movie without the subtitles.

I felt I couldn't understand what people were saying in real life, like *everything* needed subtitles. And so I replayed the sequence of events, again. My face scrunched. Matt had been about to tell me something that night and then we'd kissed. And what was all the "You've won" bullshit? What race was I in? More importantly, who was I racing against? Had I been racing against a woman with legs from her to Toledo? Well. Shit. No wonder she got to him before I did.

"Stop thinking about him," Megan said, interrupting my Zen-like flow of ideas. "Really. You're going to make yourself sick. You've got to get over him. He's gone and out. And what all of this proves was Matt wasn't The One for you. He was just emotional practice. Your real One will show up later." She said it like it was all so easy.

I nodded my head but I wasn't convinced. Weren't you only supposed to feel love once? I mean, a deep love that is both physical attraction and emotional excitement? That's what I felt for Matt; even knowing he was engaged to someone else. And there it was again. Engaged. To someone else. I just felt like the whole thing was wrong somehow.

And just because he was engaged, did that mean I should just instantly fall in love with someone else? It didn't work that way. Matt *was* the One. I was sure of it. I wouldn't have felt that way if he weren't.

"He's engaged, Chloe." Megan said. "Give me the popcorn back. I don't know why you insist on sharing. If you'd just give me my own bowl you wouldn't have to pass it."

"I know he's engaged," I said, "And if you'd let me make microwave popcorn we could each have our own bag and we wouldn't have to pass at all."

"Do you know how many toxins are in those microwave bags?" She asked, incredulously. I passed the bowl. "Like a billion toxins and then what do you do to them? You *microwave* them. Make them nuclear toxins or something."

"Isn't your leg any better? Sheesh. It's like you're becoming my roommate or something." As much as she annoyed me, I sort of liked having her around. It was sort of nice coming home and having someone to eat and talk with.

"This is the best part," Megan said and munched. "And stop thinking about him. Your brain is going to explode."

But how do you stop thinking about the love of your life? And what do you do with the hole left in the heart, the space they used to occupy? It's not like digging a hole in the sand. It doesn't immediately fill up with water when a wave washes over you. It just stays, well, a hole.

Yeah. So instead of doing anything productive, I just sat there and thought about my hole. I laughed. "My hole," I said out loud.

"I don't even want to know," Megan said and then turned the volume up.

17

A Promise of Chex Mix and Adventure

We had just finished the movie and were both working on our computers (Megan doing work for the bankruptcy law firm, me: writing a grant for the musical society) when my phone rang. Megan grabbed it for me. She was terrible on the phone. If you were a nosy type of person (which I was) then you liked to listen in on other people's conversations. I'd followed people in the mall just to find out if someone's aunt really had an affair with their neighbor or were the people talking on the phone going to agree to see a marriage counselor. You could hear all kinds of conversations by listening to one person talk into their cell. But listening to Megan didn't give you a clue as to what the conversation was actually about.

"Yeah," she said. "Okay." Pause. "Really?" Pause. "We could take our computers." Pause. "Pretty much a mess." Pause. "Okay." Pause. "Seriously Chex Mix?" Pause. "I'll tell her."

She hung up the phone, grabbed her crutches and started making her way to the spare bedroom. I followed her trying not to be obvious. When I saw her take down her giant suitcase and stuff it back with the things she'd brought over to my apartment, I got nervous.

"You don't have to go, Megan. I'm totally happy with you staying here. In fact, you could move in permanently for all I care, but just . . ." Shit. I was starting to cry. "Don't go yet. You don't have to go yet."

"*I'm* not going anywhere," she said. "*We* are. Go pack your bags."

"Pack my bags?" My heart did a little two-step, and then a pirouette and then some kind of hip hop shimmy or something.

"That was your mom. She'll be here in a half hour. We're taking The Beast on a little road trip."

A road trip? With Megan, my mom, and The Beast?

"And pack your computer. We may be gone for a few days so you might have to finish your grant on the road. You can do that right?"

I nodded dumbly. "Sure. That's what freelancing is for. So you can pick up and leave town for a while. But where are we going? And why?"

Megan stopped packing and looked at me. "Your mom said she'd tell you when she got here. And she said she was bringing Chex Mix."

My moment of worry vanished. Chex Mix! Mom was coming over and bringing Chex Mix! She was pretty much a terrible cook, but there was one thing she could make and that was anything with cereal in it.

"What are you waiting for? Go!" Megan urged.

Right. Go. Suddenly I felt focused, energized, and, well, happy.

I packed in three minutes.

18

Mom, a Beehive, and the Power of the Universe

Three hours later, we were still waiting for my mom. This is the trouble with free spirits. They're entirely unreliable! When she did show up, I could see why she needed extra time. She was swathed in scarves, had dyed her hair a purpley-red, and had it spun up in a beehive of all things. A beehive! I just stared at her.

She pooh-poohed Megan and mine expressions. "They were offering a class in Contemporary Hair and Beauty and Marla wanted to give it a try."

Contemporary? Contemporary for 1960, maybe.

"Oh, if I put sunglasses on, it's fine. I look like a movie star. Sunglasses pretty much take care of everything, don't you think?" She waited for us to say something. I was thinking that she did, actually, look like a movie star.

"Well?" I asked, getting annoyed now.

"Well, what?" She looked at me like she had no idea what I was talking about.

"Megan and I are all packed."

"And?" she said.

"And where are we going?" I tried not to sound irritated, but it was a struggle.

"Oh! Where are we going? Well well well. That is an interesting question. Let's load up The Beast, put it in drive and I'll tell you which direction to go."

"No," I said, and I knew I was really losing any sort of patience I had. "I'll tell you which direction you can go, Mom."

Megan shushed me. "Ma, tell her about what you overheard at the diner . . . with your E.S.P."

Mom smiled. Pressed two fingers to her forehead and said . . . "Ah, yes, my E.S.P." She didn't have to tell me she didn't mean Extra Sensory Perception, she meant Eavesdropping Sensory Perception. Mom was even nosier than I was. "I was at Russ's Restaurant this morning, it's where all the retirees go. Things are cheap and if you don't leave a tip they just chalk it up to Alzheimer's. When what should I hear but a certain Southerny-type accent talking to an uptight woman."

"Matt!" I gasped.

"Tell her the next part . . ." added Megan.

"And, apparently, your little heart breaker is on his way with his lady friend to Mackinac Island for some kind of race thing and I was thinking . . ."

I was already out of the door, lugging my suitcase to the car.

Mom ran after me. I could hear Megan clumping slowly down the stairs. When she caught up with me, she grabbed my hand gently and said in a very motherly fashion (which made me a little uncomfortable): "And I was thinking that you need to exorcise this man from your system! We should follow him up there so that you can say good bye and good riddance and find yourself someone who will make a decent partner, and who's fertile and with a good job so you can give me some grandbabies to play with. I just bought a giant bubble wand that I . . ."

I was already nodding my head.

But to be honest, and I'm really trying to come clean here, I didn't want to say goodbye and good riddance. I wanted to turn him away from his fiancé and have him fall in love with me. Forever and for good.

Why? Why was I thinking this way?

Remember, my mom said she thought I was conceived after she ingested too many mushrooms. Maybe that's the reason.

Or maybe because I'd spent so much time and energy in a relationship that wasn't a relationship that I was caught up in the evil power of the universe: inertia.

19

Mom's Idea of Fun

On the map of Michigan, Mackinac Island looked really close. From Grand Rapids (mid-left-hand side of the mitten) it appeared to only be an inch or so. What did an inch or so translate to in map-language?

Six hours! SIX HOURS! And I loved my mother, I really did, but she also drove me crazy. Every ten minutes she wanted to go pee. "You'll understand when you have children. They stretch out your vagina and your bladder and you're never the same."

"Mom! Eeeek! Too much information!" I cried. Really, any time a mother says the word 'vagina' it's too much information.

From the backseat, Megan offered: "We could just get you an adult diaper. Then we wouldn't have to stop so much."

I felt The Look pouring off from Mom even before she turned around to look at Megan. "I will never, ever wear an adult diaper. Now an adult bikini . . . *maybe*. But a diaper? Please." She flipped the visor down and reapplied her plum lipstick. It matched her hair perfectly. "It's time to play a game or something. I'm going out of my head."

Mom was obsessed with games. She carried a parachute and a ball in the trunk of her car just in case she entered a party and needed spontaneous entertainment. The extended car ride, I'm sure, felt like commitment on her part — not commitment to a relationship, but hospital commitment.

"All right," she said. "Let's play Therapist."

Megan swallowed a laugh in the backseat. "That's not like playing doctor is it?"

"No, dear, I'm past my experimental phase unless, of course, Gerard Butler is playing Doctor, then call me Nurse."

She sighed and looked out the window.

"Mom? The game?"

"Oh, yeah. So we can say a recurring dream we've had and then you guys be the therapist and analyze it."

And I don't know why, but this sounded like a great idea to me.

"I'll go first," Mom said. "I have this recurring dream about Matt Damon . . ."

"Coffee break!" I cried, and pulled over at Jack's Pasties & Snacks Shack, the last restaurant before the last exit to the island.

20

Of all the Pasty Shacks in Northern Michigan He Walks Into Mine

Six hours on the road gave all of us road-induced-hunger. Jack's Shack promised Breakfast All Day! and Pasties the Size of Your Head! We passed on the pasties. (Mom said: "Aren't those the twirly things they put on nipples? I already have a pair, and I hardly need more the size of my head.") Instead, Mom wisely ordered the Hippie Hash (sautéed veggies and hash brown potatoes in a skillet). It was supposed to be a healthy choice, but then she ordered bacon, Canadian bacon, and an egg and slid that on top of the hash. I had the usual: hash browns, egg over medium, wheat toast, and Megan had a gigantic cinnamon roll that was literally dripping in white frosting. Drip drip drip.

Mom took a deep breath and began: "I keep having this fantasy about Matt Damon. It's a recurring dream, really."

Megan and I chewed our food. Sometimes, especially with my mother, it was best not to say anything. My mom looked at us, and then harrumphed. "I've been having this dream over and over and in it Matt Damon picks me up and . . ." She looked at us expectantly. Megan nudged me with her elbow.

"Yes, Ms. Knaggs?" I asked, playing Therapist.

"Call me Frenchie."

"Mah-mmm." I said.

"Oh all right. Anywho . . . Matt Damon takes me to a restaurant. It's a pub really with, you know, those big oaky type walls and booths with vinyl seats. And then he orders for me."

"And?" I asked. I felt my muscles tense as I anticipated Mom using the 'vagina' word. (Couldn't they come up with a prettier word for it?) I knew she was about to give us the lurid details of I'm bracing myself of Matt Damon throwing her on the big oaky-table and . . .

Mom set her fork on the table. She took a deep breath and for an instant I was afraid she was going to tell me something dark, and deep, and disturbing, and I didn't have enough money to afford real therapy. "We have the best fish'n'chips I've ever experienced. It's really golden and fluffy and like amazing. I have vinegar with mine. He likes lemon. We don't do tartar sauce." She picked up her fork again and dug in.

Megan cocked her head and looked at me, perplexed. "Uhm . . ." she managed when it was clear my mom was done telling us about her big fantasy.

"That's it? That's your fantasy?" I said.

"Well, sometimes he orders pizza. New York style pizza. But my favorite is when he orders the fish'n'chips. Now, it's your turn. Analyze away and then I'll pretend to be your therapist."

Megan started to laugh and then tried to cover it up by taking a big ol' slurp of coffee.

"Mom, that's not a fantasy."

Mom nodded and her jewelry tinkled. "Sure it is. The fish is cod. Like, really good cod. You hardly ever get cod anymore."

After a long while, Megan opened her mouth, raised her finger as if just about to posit a theory and then said: "Holy shit!"

Because outside Jack's Pasties & Snacks Shack was a dusty motorcycle, and on that motorcycle were two leather-encased bodies: one distinctly male, and the other silicone-enhanced female. And they didn't even have to take off their helmets. We knew who they were.

Matt M. and his fiancé, Amber. In the flesh. Outside. And walking into the restaurant.

21

What Endorphins Can Make You Promise

"Oh my God. Oh my God. Oh my God!" I was hyperventilating.

Mom immediately slipped into her Yogi mode. "Chloe, try taking a breath and saying Ohmmmmm. Like this . . . Ohmmmmmm. Ohmmmm."

"Megan, what do I do?"

She looked at me, at the door, at the table, at the bathroom, and said, "Hide!"

I acted on impulse and hid in the only place I could think. Under the table. Which probably would have been fine if the place had tablecloths, but this was not a tablecloth place, this was Jack's Pasties and Snack Shack, so I cowered under a completely bare table, trying to hide behind Megan's cast encased leg.

"Oh, wow! Megan, Frenchie, and hey!" Matt bent down and smiled at me under the table. "Chloe! I thought that was you. Did you lose an eye contact or something?"

"Uhmmm . . . .Just a sec here." What was I supposed to do? How could I get out of this smoothly? I crawled out from under the table, popped up and smoothed my hair and said: "Megan had an itch. In her cast. That I scratched. With this," I held up a chopstick that had been (for some reason) on the floor.

"She's a good friend," Megan said. "She's really thoughtful like that."

Matt nodded. "I know, I know." Amber did a little chuckle that in womenspeak sounded like a chuckle that meant: how pathetic.

"Ma-tt" she sang. "I'm getting hun-gry." She strutted over to a booth in the corner and tapped her foot.

"Just a second, love. So . . . this is odd." He smiled and I looked at his lips, those lips, and I wanted to . . . He lowered his voice for a moment. "I've been trying to get a hold of you for days. When I saw you at my house, I wanted to tell you . . ."

My heart was about to orgasm. What was he going to tell me?

Amber strutted back over, calling his name, and looped her arm in his. Abruptly, his voice raised and whatever he was going to tell me went out the window. "So. Yeah. What are you doing here? I mean Jack's Shack of all places." He laughed and I wanted to punch him. In the wiener. But I was more reserved than that. I was also suddenly mute, still holding the chopstick in my hand like a weapon.

"Oh, we're going up to the *Island*," Mom said, as if Mackinac was her own personal Martha's Vineyard.

"You are? That's crazy!" He laughed and ran his hand through his sandy brown hair. "Wow. Double weird. That's where we're headed too!"

"You don't say?" asked Megan.

"So are all of you running or just Chloe? Probably not you though Megan, huh? Looks like you had an accident or something."

Wait a minute. Running? Did he just say running? Why running?

Mom didn't miss a beat. "Chloe is the only one running. She loves to run. We're her cheerleaders." Mom flashed a movie star smile and Megan said "Rah. Rah."

"*You're* running in the Blue Turtle Race?" Amber asked. And maybe it was her tone or maybe I was super sensitive but I swear she was looking at me like she didn't think I could run to get a candy bar let alone in a race.

"Well, yeah," I managed.

"Sweet!" Matt offered. "What are you running? The half marathon or the 10k?"

I blinked. I looked at Mom. She blinked. Megan scratched her leg with the chopstick. Shit. Which one was shorter? I knew in gold a Karat was like 1,000 something and that if there were ten of them . . . I did the calculations. "I'm running the half marathon," I said smugly, thinking it was the shorter of the two distances.

Amber chuckled. "Really?"

Matt exhaled. And he smiled a genuine smile. "Wow, Chloe, thirteen point one miles! I didn't even know you were a *runner*. You never told me."

I raised my chin. "Well, there's a lot you don't know about me, Matt." Take that! Part of me wanted to say, "I'm also killer at fellatio" but the presence of my mom made me resist. There are some things you just don't say in front of a mother.

He just looked at me for a second, and then shook himself like he was shaking water off his face. "Yeah. Wow.

You. Running. That's cool." Amber cleared her throat. "Well. Yeah," Matt said. "That's what we're running too. I guess we'll see you at the starting line."

We said our goodbyes and Matt followed Amber to the booth in the back, both of them sitting on one side.

"How mortifying," I said and slunk down to my seat.

"I think you handled that nicely," Megan said.

I shook my head.

"It'll be a great way to get him out of your system, Chloe. Running cleanses the chakras. And maybe you can catch up to him, tell him off or at least say you're done with him, and then we'll come home and everything will be fine." Mom said.

But I just shook my head again. "How far is a 10k?" I asked.

Megan stifled a laugh. "About 6 miles I think."

Six miles I could handle. I could run about two miles, and walk four, but thirteen! Run, walk, and crawl thirteen miles!

What, oh what, was I thinking?

Then I heard Amber's Tinker Bell laugh and saw her lean in and kiss him on his lips. Correction. She kissed him on *my* lips. Those were my lips!

"I'm going to run her into the ground." I growled.

"Ah-ah-ah," Mom warned. "Karma.'

"Karma schmarma," I said. "Let's get out of here." I had some mental training to do and I didn't think I could bear seeing them kiss again.

22

Another Brief (meaning long) Digression
In Which I Defend Myself

At this point (if not before) you might be asking yourself, how could she (meaning me, Chloe Knaggs) keep being so stupid? Wake up, lady! Clearly her relationship with Matt was only a friendship! And how could she continue to not get the point that he didn't want her when he got engaged to someone else, and by all means why on earth did she think she could prove to him that he did want her by running 13.1 miles . . . a distance she (meaning me) has never run? That's a long sentence, but I know exactly what you mean.

I was stupid, but it was a stupidity of *longing* not of brain power.

It's actually pretty easy to answer.

I met Matt when I was thirty and I simply didn't want to date anymore. I was bone tired of it all. I didn't want another man-bead on my string of relationships. I didn't want to kiss someone within moments of meeting them, go to bed with them after a few dates (or just one date), be in a relationship for a little while with someone, and then break up and start all over again. I wanted The Real Deal. And what was The Real Deal? The Real Deal was, is, a relationship that develops slowly over time. Just like he'd said to me on our fist un-date. You don't have sex right away. You wait. You don't even kiss. You can think of it either as neo-Christian Born Again Virgins or the way I like to think of it: courting old school. With Matt, I felt like I was Lizzy to his Mr. Darcy. I felt, honestly, that there was something deep between us that time was only enhancing. I believed it. Knew it for a fact. And when it wasn't a fact, I went crazy.

It's as easy as that.

23

Into the Twilight Zone

"Christ," Megan breathed, looking at the ferry rolling up to the dock. "You didn't tell me it'd be surrounded by water!"

"Uhm. It's an *island*, Megan," I said as gently as I could which wasn't all that gently because, duh, it's called Mackinac *Island*.

"I know. But I thought we were going on the Bridge. I didn't know ferries would be involved."

"I thought you always wanted to ride a fairy. Get it? F-A-I-R-Y, not F-E . . ."

"I get it. But no. It's an Elf King I'd like to ride, and not a fairy or this ferry either. Can't we just take Bridge? I thought a bridge was involved somewhere."

"The Mackinac Island Bridge connects the upper and lower peninsula. Mackinac Island is a little island between the two. The only way to reach the island is by boat."

"Huh?" Mom and Megan looked at me like I was suddenly speaking in tongues. And I wasn't, exactly, but I had just read a handy little brochure about Mackinac

Island.

"Oh, just, let's get our tickets," I said, resisting the urge to summarize the island's highlights, which were, in bullet points: the island had no motorized vehicles, but it did have haunted house, lots of fudge, and the Grand Hotel where "Somewhere in Time" was filmed. God, I loved that movie. "Did you know there are no motorized vehicles on the island?" Again, they gave me a look. "Oh, for fuck's sake. I just read a brochure." I handed it to them.

"No cars. But lots of chocolate." Megan nodded. "I can deal with that. Though I hate leaving The Beast behind."

"I agree. I'd rather take The Beast with us," Mom offered. "After all, you know what no motorized vehicles really means?" She waited for an answer. I thought it was a rhetorical question. "Horse poop. A whole lot of horse poop."

So much for my romantic vision.

We stood in line and paid like twenty bucks a piece, and then went over to another line and stood in that one. There were tons of people, so many that I was afraid we were going to have to wait for the next ferry, and I really didn't want to wait. With every passing moment, coming on this trip seemed increasingly stupid. To get my mind off the bad choices I was probably making, I looked around. No matter where you are, if you stop to look, you'll notice that people are weird. And interesting. It can make you feel a whole lot better about your own life. Especially if you see someone with really bad hair or cream cheese on his or her chin or something.

This crowd was no exception. The more I looked, in fact, the weirder the crowd became . . . weird because they all sort of looked the same. It was like we'd stumbled into a casting call for Nike. "Hey, Megan," I whispered. We'd rented a little wheelchair for her and she looked very relaxed I thought. I was pushing her and Mom was off doing typical Mom stuff. Megan's leg sticking out in front of her gave us a nice cushion of space between us and all the other passengers. "Hey, Megan!" I said louder, but trying to do it as an aside so everyone else wouldn't hear. It didn't work.

"I'm right here, sheesh. You don't have to shout. What?"

"You notice anything weird?" The line inched forward. We gazed around us.

"Yeah. Your mom is doing a headstand against the light pole."

"Oh, that. That's nothing. She's probably trying to get focused. No. Look at all the people. They look really . . . bizarre. It's like we're in L.A. or something."

Megan looked and I saw the expression on her face shift. "Holy shit," she said. "Everybody here is really skinny."

Now, I love Michigan, but the sad truth is, when two Michiganders meet, it's their bellies that greet each other before the rest of them catches up. I don't know why. Maybe it's the whole car state thing, where there's like a cultural agreement not to walk anywhere, but Michiganders are a little bit chubby. We like cheese and potatoes and not walking. But everyone lining up for the ferry . . . thin. Like tall reeds. Or an assortment of people trying out for a reality show. And everyone, men and women, were wearing Lycra or something. And tennis shoes. And t-shirts that said Boston Finisher or Marine Marathon Recruit or I Am an Iron Man. And they were doing contorted lunges and stretches in line. And then it hit me. "Megan! These people! These people are . . . *runners.*"

Abruptly the line started moving and we surged forward. "Mom! Mom!" I called.

I was reaching for my mom and somehow Megan got ahead of me. "Chloe! Chloe! I'm rolling! I can't stop!" And before I could do anything, Megan in her wheelchair that apparently had no break was rolling down the plank. All I could see were marathon runners taking dives to get out of the way. They were pretty flexible. One of them did something that I'm sure was called a Triple Bypass Monty.

And then I heard the crash.

Megan and her wheelchair were sandwiched between a running stroller and a luggage cart. "Can we go home yet?" She asked softly.

Mom pulled the stuff off her. "Megan. You are absolutely brilliant. You brought us to the head of the line!"

Megan and I turned to look. It was true. We'd gone from the back all the way to the front, and now had prime choosing for the seats in the ferry. "It was all part of my evil plan," Megan said.

With a little help from an overly cheerful teenager, we managed to get Megan up the steep stairs and onto the top deck. Once the ferry started, about an hour later, and we were crossing Lake Michigan, something peculiar happened.

Mom, Megan and I sat all in a row. The sun was shining, and the boat rocked a bumpy rhythm in the water as it picked up speed. With the motor and the loud wind and the water splashing all over us, we couldn't talk at all. We just grinned like Trekkies at a convention, and started giggling. Megan started it. Her little huh-huh-huh giggle, and then Mom started shaking and then I started laughing too with, I'm sure a snort here and there.

I'm not exactly sure why. But for that thirty-minute crossing, we just laughed and laughed and forgot about everything else. It wasn't until we got off the ferry that I noticed Matt and Amber had been with us the whole time. And he was staring at me. When Amber wasn't looking, he held up his fingers to his ear in a 'call me' gesture. I should have been excited, but the whole thing made me feel a little sick to my stomach.

It was either seeing Matt tell me to call him that made my tummy sick, or it was all the horse poop sizzling in the sun.

24

The Cost of a Free Spirit

"So where are we staying?" I asked Mom.

We'd waited until the crowd surged pats us in an amorphous blob of running shorts and shoes, and then we considered which direction to go. The Island was cuter than I expected. Picturesque Victorian Homes lined a cobblestone street and you could hear the clomp clomp clomp of actual horses pulling actual carriages. "Staying? What do you mean? How would I know? I'd like to stay in one of those houses. Maybe we could make friends with someone."

My mom in a nutshell: Plans? What plans? Let's just make friends. I couldn't bear it. "What do you mean how would you know where we're staying? You planned the trip. You called us, right? It was all your idea."

Mom scrunched her face as if flipping through her memories. "I called you on an adventure. An adventure, mind you, I'm sure psychically you were telling me to plan because you couldn't bring it up yourself. I'm just a psychic, darling. Not a travel agent."

"You mean, you didn't hook us up with a room?" What was I thinking? I'd relied on my mom to make our travel plans!

"Honey, something will turn up. I mean, it's not like this place is popular or something. There's got to be some place we can sleep for the night."

Not popular? Not popular? Shit. It was like Disney World without the stuffed characters walking around. The place was packed! And at that moment the last ferry to the mainland blew its lonely whistle. We were stranded.

"We could always stay with your friend Matt," Megan offered.

What!??!

And then I heard her snickering.

Very funny. Very fucking funny. "Come on," I said. "Let's get a drink first and then figure out where to crash."

"And then register you for your big race tomorrow," Mom added cheerily.

Yes. My big race.

I hadn't really slowed down long enough to think all of this through. Why should I start now? "To the bar!" I called.

"Onward, ho!" Megan echoed.

And so we went. Into the Ole Tally Tavern.

25

This Could Only Happen To Me

The Ole Tally Tavern was a small pub with oak floors, booths, and ceiling. Sort of what an oak womb would be like I imagine. Mom snuggled into a corner booth and I sat next to her. Megan's leg prohibited her from snuggling, so she just sat at the end of the table, turned so her leg jutted out.

"My God," Mom breathed looking around. "This is just like the restaurant in my dreams. You know the recurring one I was telling you about?"

Megan nodded. "The one where Matt Damon buys you pizza."

"Fish n chips," Mom corrected.

"Made of halibut."

"Cod," Mom and I said at once. "Because you hardly ever get cod anymore," I finished.

"I think I had an honest to goodness premonition. I've seen us here before. I think we're really onto something."

Or Mom was *on* something, I thought to myself. We picked up our menus. "Gawd," Megan breathed, trying to hoist the enormous menu up in front of her eyes. "I've heard that everything is bigger in the north . . ." She paused midsentence as our waiter materialized next to Megan. She turned her head and was nose to, well, let's just say, our waiter's lower waist. Midsection. Below the belt. To the side of the leg. Oh, for crying out loud, Megan's nose almost touched our waiter's dick (which was in his pants of course).

"Case in point," Mom said and motioned to our waiter.

"Hey," he said. We all stared at his bulge.

"Hey," we all said. And then, after a long awkward moment, I looked up at him. Megan continued to stare.

"Holy moley!" he said. "Chloe Knaggs?"

Mom smiled wide. "Look at that," she said. "What's your name?"

"Chad," he said.

"You know my daughter?"

"I sure do!" He sounded really excited.

"You don't by any chance live in one of these nice Victorian homes do you?"

"Just for the summer," he said.

Mom patted my knee in a gesture that said: See, dear, what did I tell you?

I tried to place him and then it hit me: Chad Phillips. The first boy I'd ever kissed.

What do you say when you're in a weird bar in Mackinac Island chasing after the man of your dreams, when your waiter approaches and he turns out to be the guy you had that magical/horrible first kiss with: the guy who all guys are measured up against, the guy you haven't seen in twenty years? I scratched my elbow. Stifled a weird burp-thing that sort of floated up from my stomach and rustled through my lips. "So." I drummed my fingers. "You still like Doritos?"

Megan just stared at his bulge.

26

A Brief Digression While I Explain My First Kiss
OR
Making Out With Chad, Circa 1989

I was dressed as a sailor. Not for any specific reason, really, except it was Halloween and I was at his party. The sailor part wasn't for a particular reason: I never dreamed of wearing flared pants, a striped blue shirt, and a white Popeye hat, but it's all I could come up with last minute. I didn't want to go to the party, but my friend Jessica liked Chad's brother and I was 15 and she could drive, so really I had no choice. She was dressed as a prostitute. Or a French maid. Hard to tell the difference really.

So there I was, awkwardly standing by the mysterious red punch, trying to look like I was really interested in my cuticles, and Chad sauntered over (as much as a 13 year old could saunter. Yes. 13.) "Hey," he said. (This was the standard pubescent greeting.)

"Hey," I said.

"You want to see my basement?"

"Okay." I said.

He reached for my hand (it was sweating) and led me through the throng of teenagers with bad hair and tiny mustaches to the basement. We walked through the beaded curtains, and it was like walking into a new world. There were beanbag chairs and a pool table and posters of Quiet Riot on the wall. "Those are my brother's," he said, explaining it all.

"Yeah," I said. We nodded because we understood each other.

"I like this kind of music better." He pushed play on the preloaded cassette player. It was the soundtrack to The Breakfast Club.

"God! I love the Breakfast Club!" I said. And I did. They ran it constantly on our local station, but dubbed out all the naughty parts so the Geek said something like "Eat my Socks," and the loser said, "Fudge you!"

"Yeah," he said. We listened. He sat on a red beanbag chair and it made a farting sound. I pretended to look at my cuticles again. "Come here," he said and offered me his hand.

I'd never sat on a boy's lap and I was terrified of squashing him, but he didn't seem to mind. He was breathing; in fact, he leaned in and suddenly his tongue was in my mouth.

Odd.

It was like kissing a beaver tail, all big and gloppy and wet and slightly disturbing. It went on for almost all of "Don't You Forget About Me." I felt okay. Mildly tingly, mildly nauseated. When the song was over, he looked at me and said, "There are Doritos upstairs. You want some?"

"Yeah!" I said my heart bursting. "I love Doritos!"

"I love Doritos too," he said, and we nodded because we understood each other. Totally.

27

An Awkward Conversation Followed By Bliss

"Do I still like Doritos?" he laughed. "I'm more into vegetable chips and soy burgers now."

Oh. A vegetarian. That was sexy.

"I'm an omnivore," barked Megan. "I eat whatever I can, whenever I can." I stared at her. She was acting really weird.

"Oh an equal opportunist, eh? That's okay with me. I'm not really vegetarian. I just like vegetables."

"Oh," Megan said and stared at her leg.

"Tell me . . . are you an Aquarius?" Mom asked.

"I am actually!" he said and before he could go on, or before my mom could go on, or before Megan's head spun around and she started frothing at the mouth, I stopped him.

"Look, Chad, we've been on the road all day, my heart is broken, we're starving and thirsty, Megan's leg itches, my mom needs her chakras cleansed, we have no where to sleep tonight and I'm running thirteen miles in two days for the first time in my life."

"Thirteen point one." Megan corrected.

"Thirteen point one. So before I break down into hysterical sobbing, could you bring us all something to drink? Whatever you think would fit the situation. I'm not choosy."

"She's really not choosy." Mom agreed.

"Leave it all up to me," he said and smiled. Then he was gone. I felt strangely comforted, like he really would take care of everything.

"That's an Aquarius for you," Mom said.

Three minutes later, Chad was back carrying a tray with three very tall glasses filled with muddy looking water. He set the drinks in front of us. "There's only one drink for you ladies tonight," he said. "The Flaming Turtle."

Then he set the drinks on fire.

After that . . . everything was pretty much a blur.

28

Why A Morning-After Is Overrated

The first thing I thought was "Oh! That feels nice." The second thing I thought was "Eek! Who is touching me! What is touching me??" I awoke to find a gigantic dog (surely a genetic relation to the Sasquatch) licking my toes. And it felt good! It felt goooooooooooooood.

I was so ashamed.

"Where the fuck am I?" I asked and looked around. It took awhile for my vision to clear. I was in an apartment, or a house, sitting on what? A hard couch? A pool table? Oh. The floor.

Then it occurred to me that I didn't know where my mom or Megan were. And Matt? I wasn't thinking about Matt. I was being sexually assaulted by a gigantic sheepdog (and I liked it!). "Megan? Mahahahahaha-hahahm?" I called. The dog stopped its licking, turned and ran, disappearing behind a corner.

And that's when I saw it.

A scarf here. A vest here. A sequined purple sweatshirt there. And what was that? A cast? Oh. It wasn't a cast. But a tube sock. A tube sock? What the? Good God! Were Mom and Megan in bed together, naked, free and wearing only one a tube sock?

Something like that.

Only my mom wasn't involved. Just Megan and my first boyfriend, Chad, doing some kind of naked interpretive dance on a futon. The only way I knew it was Megan was by the white cast of her leg extending straight up in the air. She really was very flexible.

"Uhm . . . excuse me?" I ventured. Their heads popped out from under a black silky sheet. "Have either of you seen my mom?"

Megan tried to smooth her hair. "Oh. Yeah. Outside. Doing her tae kwon do."

"Tai Chi," Chad corrected.

"Right. Tai Chi."

"Okay. Thanks there, Megan, and ehm . . . Chad."

Chad smiled. "Sure thing!" He said. And then he was back under the cover doing God knows what.

Megan shushed me and gave me a, "I know, I know" look. I silently shut the door, and followed the trail of my mom's clothes out onto the patio where, yes, she was as naked as the morning, raising her hands to mother moon and father sun, crying (as Miss Piggy did all those years ago) "Hiiiiiya!!!"

29

Mom, In The Buff

"Mom!" I cried. Do I need to say I was horrified? "Mom! Come on!"

Mom looked at me and smiled. "Good morning, sunshine! Care to join me?"

"No. Good God. No! Where are your clothes?"

She stretched her arms way above her head and I shut my eyes. There are just some things you don't want to know about your mother. Finding out that she's recently had a breast lift is one of them. "Clothes, schmoes," she said. "That was some night last night, huh?"

"Huh?" I shook my head. Nodded. I had no clue.

"You don't have a clue, do you?" she asked and then laughed. "You can open your eyes now, honey. I've covered my shame."

I opened my eyes. She was wearing a gigantic red terrycloth robe on it that said: "Sun & Fun Mackinac is #1!" Where did she find these things?

"I wasn't trying to make you feel shame about your body, Mom, it's just . . ."

"I know. Boundaries. *Boundaries.*" She raised her hand in a gesture that told me it was all water under the bridge. "So are Megan and Chad still . . ."

"Dancing in the moonlight?" I asked. "Yes."

"Good. Then let's go have breakfast. I'm famished. And I can tell you all about all the crazy things you did last night."

Crazy things? Did I do crazy things? I didn't recall anything crazy. I'm not really a crazy type of person. And then, something tickled my mind. Some image of me standing on top of a table and . . . "Sweet Buddha," I breathed.

"It's all coming back to you, isn't it?" Mom said sympathetically. "Best wait until you've eaten until you remember everything. Otherwise you might make yourself faint. And we don't want to have to get Matt to carry you to bed. Again."

Matt? Carry me? To bed? What the . . . Was that all he had done? Damn you Flaming Turtles! Damn you!!! "Did he really carry me to bed? Mom? Mom!" I called, but she had already dropped the robe and was picking up pieces of her clothes and dressing. I waited for my head to clear and my heart to stop pounding before I followed her inside.

30

It's All Coming Back To Me Now

I followed Mom out the door and onto the front porch of a great yellow Victorian House on the top of a green, green hill. "Wow," I said.

Mom stood next me, shoulder to shoulder. "Sort of makes you want to take off your clothes and say a bit of praise, doesn't it?"

I nodded dumbly. It was beautiful. Below us, was the quaint Mackinac Island town, appearing as it had a hundred years ago: thin streets lined with brightly colored gingerbread homes. A horse and carriage passed by us, the horse clomping slowly forward. The driver waved. And beyond the houses and carriage, there waited Lake Michigan. Beautiful, blue, as big as a sea. I breathed in deeply, feeling the tension and confusion slip away from me as easily as if I had disrobed.

"You ready?" Mom asked.

I nodded.

"Good. Then as we're walking, you can try to remember about that kiss."

Mom started walking down the hill briskly and I just stared. Boy. She really had a knack for getting me to follow her. What kiss? What kiss? What did I do?

And then I remembered.

Matt M. Of course. Mmmmm. Love of my life, of my fantasies. I'd kissed him again. Right in front of Amber.

***

Mom chomped on a celery stalk from her Bloody Mary, her 'cure all hangover cure, with antioxidants in the tomato juice'. "So, is it all coming back to you?" she asked.

"Yeah. It is. Ugh."

"Well, one good thing. He didn't carry you home. Chad did. You passed out around 2 am."

I breathed a sigh of relief. At least I was clear on that . . . but there was still plenty to regret. "Mom, why . . . why do I get myself into situations like these?"

She looked at me and smiled then wiped the hair away from my eyes. "Such a pretty face," she said as if this remotely answered my question. "You're just like me. You have the curse of being interesting."

"Or stupid."

"Interesting. So many other people out there are afraid to do anything different, and you, you just embrace different all over the place."

"I'm a mess. It's like I have super powers for messing up my life. Just call me Blunder Woman."

Mom nodded. "At least it's not Boring Woman. Do you need me to refresh your memory about last night?"

I shook my head. No. I remembered everything now.

31

Flaming Turtle #1

Chad put the drinks in front of us. "There's only one drink for you ladies tonight," he said. "The Flaming Turtle." They were served in shot glasses rimmed in melted caramel and looked like thick chocolate sludge.

Then he set them on fire. They burned and bubbled like drinks poured from a cauldron. "I feel like I should say an incantation," Mom said.

"Maybe you should," Megan offered.

"All right. May tonight live in infamy."

"Amen!" I said. We blew out our drinks and then . . . down the hatch.

"Yummy. Minty. Chocolaty and what else is that flavor?" asked Megan, as she licked her lips trying to figure it out.

"That lingering flavor is called alcohol and a whole lot of it. Chad, dear, bring another round!"

Flaming Turtle #2

"Do you think this is a good idea?" I asked, holding the second Flaming Turtle in my hand.

"It's a swell idea, dear. Don't you think, Megan? Thank you Chad."

"I think it's a swell idea. Down the hatch!"

Down they went.

Yum. I was feeling very relaxed.

Flaming Turtle #3

Chad brought us another round. "Why don't you guys hang out for a little longer? I'll be finished with my shift in about twenty minutes." He winked at us and then walked away from the table. Megan blew out her drink, took a sip and then said: "I hate him."

"Why would you hate him?" I asked. "You don't even know him."

"You don't either."

"Sure I do. I made out with him once."

"And that qualifies as knowing someone?"

"Sure. If I remember correctly, he was a good kisser."

"Hardly a personality test. He might have been harmless as a teenager but he could be a homicidal-split-personality-bi-polar-bulimic now."

"Yeah. But at least he has good hygiene." We could all agree on that. Chad smelled good. And clean. And minty fresh.

"I hate him," Megan said again. I tried to get her to look at me but she just studied the writing on her cast, tracing it with her finger. Megan never hated anyone. Scratch that. The only person she's ever hated was Eric, and she'd been engaged to him. I took a deeper look at her. Her cheeks were flushed and she was breathing shallow, and it hit me, the way it hits you when you know something. Megan was attracted to Chad. Crazy inexplicably attracted. And she was afraid that he wanted me instead.

I took another sip of my drink. "I love Flaming Turtles," I said. "And I'm not interested in Chad." Megan wouldn't look at me. "And I don't think he's interested in me either. It's you he's been staring at all evening."

"Oh, he is not," Megan grumbled.

Mom took a sip of her drink. "Then what do you call that?" She motioned to the bar and there was Chad, staring.

"Christ," Megan breathed. "He's really beautiful isn't he? I think I'm in love with him."

Down the hatch!

Flaming Turtle #4

I loved my mom and Megan. I loved everybody. I even loved Chad. I especially loved Chad because he and Megan were making out right at the table and wasn't that interesting? Watching their pheromones bounce off each other and oh, I felt good, nice a warm and bubbly and smooth like melted chocolate. "I love you Mom. I'm so glad you're here."

"I love you, Chloe. I'm so glad I housed you in my womb."

"I'm glad too. I love your womb."

"I love my womb too. I'm going to make a sweatshirt that says that. I could probably sell it. Make enough to pay for the next decade at the retirement village."

"That's a great idea."

"You know what else is a great idea?" Mom asked.

"What's that?"

"Grandbabies. Why don't you use your womb and grow me some grandbabies?"

"I'll get right on that." I smiled. Watched Megan and Chad making out. Watched all the people in the bar laughing and loving and looking so happy. Boy, the world really was a neat kind of place. Everyone seemed happy, even that couple walking in together arm and arm, looking for a place to sit, coming straight at us. Straight at me.

"Holy shit!" I said. "It's Mmmmmm. Mmmmmmm!"

Chad took a break and looked at me. "Is she stuttering?" he asked Megan. Megan shook her head.

"No. That's Mmmmm. Matt. He broke her heart."

"He's breaking it still," I said.

Down the hatch.

Flaming Turtle #5

"I hate my life. I hate my life! I'm doomed. Dooooooomed!!!" I was crying. Actual tears cascading down my face, and then I felt a warmth on my shoulder. I turned and there was Matt looking at me, his hand on my shoulder. "Hey, now, Chloe, are you okay?"

"Am I okay? Am I Okay? I'll show you okay!" And then I leapt at him.

Imagine an octopus devouring its prey.

That was me, and Matt was my prey. I was sucking his face like I could vacuum it right up. I swear the entire bar quieted to a hush. All I could hear was the pounding of my heart and, yes, my loins. The kiss lasted two days, or a second, depending on your perspective. And then there was a pressure on my stomach. What was that? Oh. That was Matt pushing me away.

"God!" Amber cried. And then she was really crying too, big old tears, and she was running out the restaurant and down the street.

Matt just looked at me. And then he looked at her. And then he went after her.

"Oh, God, what did I do?" I cried. "Why did I do that? Why??"

And then another drink appeared before me. Magically. I blew it out like a birthday candle, made my wish, and then . . . yes . . . down the hatch.

32

Flaming Turtles 1-5
Revisited

"BWAAAAAAAH! BWAAAAAAAAAH!!!"

Uhm. Yes. That was me. In the bathroom. Puking.

Mom patted my back. "There, there, Chloe. It's all right. Get all those toxins and anxieties out of your system."

I looked up at her. I was sitting on my knees in front of the restaurant's toilet. "I'm not throwing up anxieties, Mom. I'm throwing up Flaming Turtles."

"Same difference," she said. She offered her hand to help me up. "I've got just the thing for you." She rummaged in her purse and handed me two ibuprofen and a travel toothbrush with toothpaste already in it. "Bingo gets crazy sometimes. I never know where I'm going to end up."

I brushed my teeth then popped the ibuprofen all while my mom rubbed my back and sang OOOOHHHHMMM sticking to a healing (aka annoying) single note. Still, it was moments like that, when Mom was taking care of me and seemed to have everything I needed in her enormous purse, that I realized I was sort of sweet on her. "I should make you a sweatshirt with World's Coolest Mom on it."

"You already did. When you were ten. I still have it, though it might be a little tight since my breast lift . . ."

"TMI, Mom. Too much." I held up my hand to emphasize that, again, there were just certain things you didn't want to hear from your parental unit.

We walked back out into the bar and everything looked sort of hazy and weird.

And then I realized I was wearing glasses.

"Whose are these?" I asked, taking them off. Mom grabbed them and put them in her purse.

"I'm not sure but they may come in handy." She said something else then but I couldn't focus, either because there were still too many residual Turtles floating in my system, or the fact that Matt M. had just walked into the restaurant. Again.

And this time he was alone.

33

A Conversation Worthy Of A Lifetime Movie

"Oh, Christ!" I breathed.

"Really?" And then Mom looked around like she was actually looking for the return of Jesus.

"The glasses! Quick!" I said, thinking I could put on a pair of glasses and like Superman transform into someone entirely unrecognizable.

"Hey Chloe. Mind if we talk?" Too late. Matt had recognized me.

I nodded dumbly.

Why was it that every time I was around him my IQ took a nosedive into the single digits? Why, why couldn't I come up with something smart and pithy, something besides, "Sure, Matt. Mmmmmm. Matt M. Talk. Drink. Talkdrink. Whatever you want."

"I think just the talk will be fine." He put his hand on my shoulder and led me into the back of the bar. I didn't have to look behind me to feel Mom and Megan and now Chad staring at us as if I were a Dead Man Walking.

We sat at a booth in the back, tucked comfortably in

the shadows. If this were any other time, I'd be thinking about just what I could do with him in the shadows, but right then, I felt . . . sort of . . . well . . . ashamed of myself.

"Hi," he said.

"Hi," I whispered. I grabbed a napkin and started fiddling with it. Oh, wasn't this interesting? If I tore it into little bits and twisted it and put it in a big pile it looked just like . . .

"Chloe? Will you even look at me?"

It looked just like a pile of napkin shreds. I looked at him.

"Here," he said. And then handed me another napkin.

"Oh, I don't need another one. Destroying one is enough."

"It's not for tearing into pieces, it's for this." And then he reached across the table and touched one of the many tears that were just cascading down my face. Damn.

"Okay," I said. I wiped my eyes. Blew my nose. Sniffled. Burped. Very attractive. All I needed was a really big fart and I'd feel 100% pathetic.

"Chloe?" he said again, softly.

I looked at him. Really looked at him. There were his lips, which were just his lips, not mine at all, and his deep brown eyes, and his crooked smile, and his hair that always looked just on the edge of crazy. "I'm sorry," I blurted. "I'm really incredibly sorry. I don't know what's come over me, I just . . ."

"I know," he said. "It's okay. I'm sorry too. I don't blame you, you know."

"You don't?"

"I wanted to tell you, Chloe, but we never . . . shit. We

were just friends and life with Amber was, is . . . just complicated and . . ." He tried on a smile. It looked too big for him. "We were just friends," he said. "I never thought . . ."

And that's when I stopped crying and I got angry. "No. You didn't think, did you? And don't tell me we were just friends. *Just* friends don't cuddle on a Sunday morning and watch movies. They don't call each other every hour and say "I'm thinking about you". They don't make plans for where they'll go on vacation. And they don't fucking marry someone else." Well, yes, that last bit didn't make sense because 'just friends' do marry someone else, don't they? "Just tell me this . . . did she send you in here to get rid of me?"

He shook his head. "I wanted to talk to you. I needed to talk to you, to tell you . . ."

"To tell me what? To tell me what??" He'd been wanting to tell me something ever since that blasted party. "Please, tell me! I mean after your party and our kiss . . . I'm really confused . . . what about that?"

"That was before. I thought . . . then . . . It was before . . ."

"Before WHAT?" My Irritated-Meter was hovering in the red space.

"Before Amber came back. We'd been broken up for a while, since you and I became friends actually, and I thought the night of the party. The kiss?" He looked at me and I could see his mouth forming a little smile. "It was a really nice kiss."

"Yes," I breathed. I actually did breathe it out, like finally I wasn't going crazy. I hadn't imagined everything. "It was a nice kiss. But that's all. We can't . . . can't we . . .

Why couldn't he finish a fucking sentence???

"Why can't we be friends?" I offered, sarcasm dripping like caramel from an apple. "Is that what you wanted to tell me all this time?"

There was a pause here where my courage slinked into a deep hole.

He looked down at his hands. "Yeah. That's what I want. I don't want to lose you, but Amber is going to be . . . she pretty much is . . . my life."

Ah.

And there it was.

That wasn't so bad. Just a little bit of devastating.

"Chloe," he began and his voice was gentle and kind and made me want to die, "Amber is . . . my *obsession*. She always has been, since high school. On the night of the party, I thought I could get over her and I almost tried, but then later, she came over and . . . well. And she finally wants me. Can you believe that? She wants me. Do you know what that feels like? When the person you've fantasized about your whole life suddenly wants *you*?"

I looked at him for a beat, not breathing. And then I said: "No. I don't know what that's like. I don't have any idea what that must feel like."

"But if you just got to know each other . . . You'd see how great she is and I know she'd love you. There's no reason why this can't work out. I never meant to hurt you. Tried to be pretty clear about my feelings."

Clear? He tried to be clear? As clear as mud, maybe. But . . .

Fuck it.

Slowly, painfully I got up from the booth, tilted my

head into the air and walked away from him, my heart thundering with every step of distance between us.

34

Bitter Truth
The Way I Imagine Arsenic Must Taste

"You remember everything now, dear?" Mom asked gently. We'd just finished our enormous breakfast and I sat back in my chair and rubbed my full Buddha belly.

"Yes. I remember now. It's really depressing, isn't it?"

"Depressing? What's depressing about it? You were grand. And you accomplished your goal. You've finally gotten that nasty character out of your life!"

"I didn't want him out, Mom. I wanted him in. Like, forever. Like those grandbabies you keep mentioning . . ."

"Oh, Chloe. Not with him. Not with that Matt fellow. He's not good enough for you."

I looked at my mom and just blinked. Not good enough for me? He was perfect for me. I wasn't good enough for him! That's what he told me in effect. That I might have been okay, but Amber . . . she was better.

Mom rummaged in her purse, grabbed some bills and slapped them on the bill. "What now, dear? Do we pick up Megan and make a run for it?"

I *could* make a run for it. That sounded appetizing. Really appetizing. We could just escape. Pretend like the entire weekend never happened, or reduce the weekend to funny stories we'd tell in the distant future. "Oh, Chloe! Remember how you got sick on Flaming Turtles?" or "Oh, Megan, remember you sucked face and then locked loins with Chad my first love?" or "Oh, Chloe, remember that silly Matt buck." "Matt who?" Hahahahahahaha.

Yeah. That sounded good. Better than good. It sounded great.

And then I said: "Mom, I *am* going to make a run for it. I want to run the turtle race tomorrow. All thirteen point one miles of it." Mom just stared at me. For a minute I just stared at me. What was I thinking? What was I saying? Did I mean it?

Yes.

I did.

I said I was going to run that stupid race and I wanted to run that race. More than anything, I wanted to finish that race and then be done with everything. It would be just one more thing to laugh about in the future, when all of this magically transformed into a funny episode in my life and not a tragedy.

"Good, dear," said Mom, not phased a bit. "Then let's go rescue Megan. If she stays with that Chad any longer he may propose to her. And we wouldn't want that, would we?"

God. Lose Megan? We certainly wouldn't want that.

35

Therapy is Serious Business
Or
Talking While a Horse Does Its Business

The three of us were lodged in the back of a horse and buggy. I'd decided we needed to scope out the course that I was doomed to run in just seven short hours. Since I didn't want to walk it, we'd decided on the fastest transportation we could find: an old horse with an old coachman, pulling an equally old, but cute, carriage. It was all very Pride And Prejudice.

When I watched historical BBC romances, trudging along in a horse and carriage always seemed so, well, *romantic.* I could just imagine being whisked off around the countryside to the pleasing clomping of horses while my virile young man tried not to touch me all the while the not-touching made me want to touch him even more more. It was very hot, in a repressed sort of way.

The truth of an actual horse and buggy ride (sandwiched between your hot-flashing mother and your hung-over best friend) is something all together different.

We had an up-close and personal view of the horse's ass, its tail lifted up exposing its puckered . . . well . . . do I have to go into details? Okay. Yes. It's puckered anus. That's harsh, but it's the truth. There ain't nothing pretty about a horse's anus. Except maybe the color. It's pink.

"I think she's going to blow!" I said, pointing to our horse.

"If our horse blows, then I'm going to blow," Megan said.

"You do look a little green."

"I blame those flaming turtles."

"Don't we all," Mom said.

"Why, oh why did I do that?" Megan said for the fifteenth time. She shook her head. I knew what she meant. I was asking myself the same thing when I thought about last night.

"I don't even know how you did all of, ehm, *that* with your leg and all," I said, meaning of course, that I didn't know how she'd done *Chad* with her broken leg and all. She was very flexible.

"Gawd. Chad. My leg." Megan's green shade deepened. "Please don't. I can't bear thinking about any of that. Can't we get this horse and carriage to take us off the island? I'm feeling really claustrophobic right now."

"That reminds me," Mom said and then rummaged in her gigantic purse. She pulled out an enormous Ziploc bag of her homemade amped-up Chex Mix. "We never did finish our game of Therapist. Let's play it now." She opened the bag and handed it to me. The scent of garlic and butter and hot horse blended in the air. It actually smelled pretty good, and I needed the calories. I was carbo loading. Our three hands dug in.

"How does claustrophobia remind you of our therapist game?" I asked between mouthfuls. CrunchCrunchCrunch. Mom looked at me in that condescending way that said way more than words. "Oh. Okay." I said after a moment, trying to think like my mom's logic, or unlogic. "I get it. Claustrophobia. Phobias. Therapist."

"Exactly," Mom said. "Now I'd just told you two about my recurring dream about Matt Damon and I'm still waiting for my analysis." She looked at us expectantly. She really was waiting for some kind of free epiphany.

"That's easy," said Megan and then she yawned. "Matt represents your yearning not for sexual fulfillment, you've had plenty of that, but for something deeper. You're yearning not for fish 'n' chips per se, but something rare, something like cod, or New York style pizza when you're hundreds of miles away. I think you want grandchildren."

I gulped. There was a long silence that stretched out. It would be the perfect time for a horse fart, but the horse didn't cooperate. "Dear Megan. You're brilliant!" Mom explained. And then she actually reached over me and handed Megan a dollar.

"Mom, did you pay her to say that?"

"Just the part about grandchildren. The rest was pure improv on her part. Very good Megan."

"Thanks."

I rolled my eyes.

"And now it's your turn Megan. Tell us about a recurring dream or issue you're dealing with."

I didn't think Megan was going to say anything. She had one of those prolonged silences. Mom didn't sway though; she just looked at Megan expectantly, using her witch powers on her or something.

"I dream about Eric," Megan said, and her voice was soft and sad, and she looked away from us. "I used to spend every weekend and holiday with him and his family. You remember," she said.

I nodded. I was sort of in shock. They'd been planning a wedding and everything, then Megan abruptly broke it off a year ago, and never uttered a word about it or him. Not to me, not to anyone. It was a subject we never talked about, although I tried to open the door to it. "What happens in the dream?" I asked.

"Nothing happens. Not really. I mean we all sit down and it's Thanksgiving or something, I mean, the house is decorated and everyone is wearing one of his mom's terrible hand knitted sweaters, and there's an enormous turkey and I'm sitting there with Eric and I feel . . . warm. Happy. And then I notice this cute little kid next to me and I reach over and wipe his face with a napkin and he looks up at me and says 'Thanks Mom'. And then I wake up."

Clomp clomp clomp.

I didn't want to play therapist anymore. It was a terrible, terrible dream. Of things that might have been. The dream of things that weren't.

"Hmmmm," said Mom. I glared at her to see that she was looking particularly Freudian, nodding her head, turning over the dream in her mind. Could she be so insensitive? Megan's heart was breaking here. It was terrible. "Clearly, you were never in love with Eric, you were in love with his family, with the idea of family, and you want a family, just not with him."

I thought Megan was going to ralph right then and there, but she turned to us and smiled this beatific smile. "Yes!" she said. "Exactly! That's why I broke up with him!"

I couldn't believe this! Megan just completely spilled her heart out. And the worst part of it was . . . that in the whole year since she'd broken up with him, I never even knew the truth. My mom found out in precisely two minutes.

"Good job, dear," Mom said. "Now it's time to get over it." She said this as if it were the easiest thing in the world, to just 'get over' heartbreak.

"Okay," Megan said and then dug her hand in the bag of Chex Mix again.

I tried to harrumph to show my frustration, but I don't think they heard me. The horse had finally *blown*.

36

Interlude
(A smart way of saying a meandering break)

It took forever to make it around the course. We went around the island, following a road along the coast. It was beautiful, rocky at the shore with blue, blue water, lined by Victorian homes and the old barracks on the hill. I couldn't believe I was going to run this. I could run four miles, tops, but thirteen? Point one? I knew it was stupid so what was the point?

Matt was the point. Amber was the point. I was the point. I said I was going to do it, and like in Horton Hears a Who, an elephant means what he says one hundred percent.

Yes. I just referred to myself as an elephant. Ugh.

I stopped the game of Therapist before it got to me, and the three of us fell into a peculiar silence. Peculiar for us anyway. Mom didn't even 'ohhhhhm' or anything, and Megan looked so relaxed she looked asleep. She was asleep! Which made sense after her acrobatics the night before. And what was there for me to do? I could replay old memories or I could fantasize. Mmmmmmmm. That was an easy one.

***

"Are you dreaming or fantasizing?" Mom asked. She jabbed me awake with one of her purple painted fingernails.

We were stopped on Main Street and there was a swarm of people around us. I stretched and moaned in a way that I hoped wasn't too suggestive

"Ah, fantasizing," Mom said. "Let's get out of here. These people are looking at us like we're steak and they're Texans." Mom was right. The tourists around us did look violent. They wanted in the carriage and they were serious about it. They were carrying pitchforks and torches and chanting "Get out! Get out!"

Well, maybe not exactly, but close.

We scrambled out as best we could without breaking Megan's other leg. She put her arms around mom and my shoulder and we just sort of stood on the sidewalk, breathing.

"Now what?" Megan asked.

I sighed. A very good question. We couldn't go drinking because it was only eleven in the morning and I was supposed to run a half marathon at dusk, and I was still full from breakfast, so what could we do?

That's when we heard the screaming.

Seriously. Real screaming.

Real screaming coming from the unreal Haunted House that we were standing in front of. "It's either get some fudge or tour the haunted house," I said.

"Hmmmm," Mom said. "Let's do both."

You wouldn't think that touring a haunted house while

eating Mackinac Island Fudge would go together, but it was sort of like chocolate dipped pretzels: a little bit crunchy and a little bit sweet, and just weird enough to freak you out.

37

A Brief Digression of Further Defense

Before I tell you the rest of what happened up there, I'm going to plead a little in self-defense.

Member of the Jury, I ask you, who hasn't made a really stupid choice once in their lives? Who hasn't been so consumed by love or lust or a combination of the two that they'd do almost anything? Who hasn't punched their love-interests' fiancé after running a half marathon and then got thrown in a 19th century barracks cell and then had their mom and best friends (dressed as giant turtles) try to spring them? Hmmm? Anybody? Anybody?

Okay then. Maybe it was just me. Just another string of blunders in my, Chloe Knaggs', twisted life.

Still, I still think I'm one hundred percent normal in this situation.

I rest my case.

38

The Run

There were about 2,000 people on Mackinac Island that spring evening, and all of them (save for my mom, Megan and Chad) were running in the damned race. I was sandwiched in at the starting gate, which was really a starting rope. It was like riding the subway in New York at rush hour, complete with ghost-groping of your rear end. "Hey!" I said to the bald guy behind me, but he just gave me the "Who me?" look.

I was not ready for this. We were going to start running in just five minutes and not only was I terribly unprepared for the drama that was about to happen, I wasn't dressed for it either. I was wearing the only thing we could come up with on such short notice: A t-shirt that read U.P. Yours (as in Upper Peninsula, a Michigander joke), a pair of puce colored shorts that were the only thing left on the sale racks, long men's brown dress socks, and my mom's purple bandit tennis shoes.

"You running for a charity or something?" The bald groper guy behind me asked.

"Yeah," I said, and pointed to my shirt.

I looked around. I couldn't find Megan or my mom anywhere. They'd promised to be there with me every step of the way and then Chad had shown up and they disappeared. Without them with me, I felt really alone.

I felt even more alone when I heard that low, musical voice calling my name: "Chloe! Hey, Chloe!"

Matt. Fucking Matt! And his fiancé! They sidled up next to me. Why would he do that?

"Some night last night, huh?" he joked. "Don't worry about it." He said and then smiled. Shitball. He was still hoping we could All Be Friends.

Amber and I knew the score. She lifted her leg into the air and pulled it to touch her head. "I was a dancer in college," she informed me. "I see you're really going to try and run this?"

"Of course she is!" Matt said. "She's tough!"

"Tough schmuff," I said. And then I blushed to my toes.

Why did they even come near me? But that was Matt. He had such a big heart that he was absolutely clueless at times.

I tried not to look at Amber but it was hard: she was gorgeous. She was wearing a cute little running skirt with a matching pink top, her brown hair was pulled in a sleek pony tail, and she was wearing (I swear to God) Manolu running shoes. She also had that perky pert perfect dancer's body: all sinew and long lines and no boobs that looked chic in a clingy shirt. My boobs looked like I was lactating.

I tried to focus on myself. To turn inward, as my mom would say. Apparently, when you're in a Zen sort of space, you can sort of tune out the entire world around you and sort of levitate. I opened my eyes to see if I was levitating. I wasn't. The ground was still firmly beneath me.

"You here on your own?" the bald guy asked me.

"Nope," Matt said. "She's here with us." He smiled at the guy and then said distinctly "Back off."

"Whoa, I was just wondering, man." The bald guy squirmed past three other people and we all moved forward.

"I don't know why you insist on doing this," Amber said.

Was she talking to me or to Matt?

"I mean it's clear you're not an athlete. I'm mean, sheesh, just look at you." Ah. So. She was talking to me. She looked me over from head to toe with the penetrating female glare that said I'm Better Than You Are.

"How about a little decency, would you Amber?" Matt said.

Wait a minute.

I sniffed the air.

What was that smell wafting toward me, besides Amber's perfume?

Was this the scent of annoyance? Of Matt's annoyance? Were he and Amber fighting?

A woman with an enormous baby growing in her belly, climbed up a rickety ladder and put a bullhorn to her lips: "Ladies and Gentlemen! The 1st Annual Mackinac Island Great Turtle Race is about to Begin. We'll count down, and when you hear the starting gun, run like the wind!!" She was incredibly peppy for being so pregnant. "And don't forget to follow the blue line. The blue line is for half marathoners. If you follow the white line you'll just have to run to Greece." There was a wave of nervous laughter.

Fuck.

"Ten, nine, eight . . ."

Shit.

"Seven, six, five . . ."

Amber pressed her perfect lips to my ears "You're going to burn, baby," she said.

"Four, three, two . . ."

I cracked my knuckles.

KABLAM!

Holy shit! What was that? Did I just have a heart attack? Is someone shooting? Did that bald guy just try to assassinate me? Oh wait a minute. They said there'd be a starting gun.

Starting gun!

What was I doing? Run, Chloe Knaggs, RUN!!!!

And against my better judgment, I did.

39

The Run . . .
Continued

Now I know why they called it the Great Turtle Race. What was that phrase? We were off like a herd of turtles. All going in the same direction, limbs flopping, and moving incredibly slowly. I thought when you heard the starting gun you were supposed to run as fast as you could. A grandmother could beat me at that pace. My grandmother could beat me, and she was dead.

"How do you like it so far?" Matt asked.

"It's okay," I said. Honestly, we weren't even running, not even walking. Really we were lollygagging.

"It'll clear out at the bend in the road." He said and smiled. Amber huffed next to him. Honestly, I couldn't blame her. If he were my fiancé and he was talking to some other girl on the race, I'd be pissed. I actually felt a tinge of sympathy for her and then she said: "Yeah. At the bend, that's where they weed out the losers from the winners."

"Will it take that long to figure out? Because it's clear

to me who's a winner already." I asked.

"Who? You?" she asked with poison just dripping from her mouth.

"No. I'm pretty sure *they* are. Or at least in my book, they are." I pointed at the two women dressed as enormous turtles, one of whom had a broken flipper and was sitting in a wheelchair.

Mom and Megan held a sign that said "Chloe Knaggs. Blunder Woman. Our Hero."

Chad was holding out a cup of water just for me.

"See you," I said, and then I sped up.

I was really running.

I couldn't let my fans down.

***

"Chloe! Chloeeeeeeeeeee!" Chad was jumping up and down and my water was splashing in its meager little cup. "Go go go!" chanted Mom and Megan. They looked like they were trying to lift their arms, but the enormous foamy turtle costumes were constricting them. They moved more like penguins than turtles.

I grabbed the water from Chad and tossed it on my head. Wasn't that what they did in marathons? True, in a marathon they were probably getting water after running a few miles, where I'd only been running a few feet. About fifty feet to be exact, but I was feeling a little parched. I stopped to drink the water and was passingly aware of Amber zooming past followed by Matt who gave me a thumbs' up sign.

"What are you guys doing? And do I need to ask about the costumes?"

"It's a closed course," Chad said. "Spectators aren't allowed. But I'm connected."

"He hooked us up as volunteers. Which came with this lovely outfit." Megan said this with zero emotion in her voice, like, I imagined, a depressed turtle would sound like.

"Why aren't you wearing a costume?" I asked Chad.

"Oh, I am," he said. "Only that comes later."

"Don't ask," Megan said.

"What are you doing, Chloe? Aren't you supposed to be running?" Mom asked then swatted my butt with her flipper. Both things were disturbing.

"Right," I said. "Run run run. Go go go."

"Rah. Rah." Said Megan.

"I'll see you at the end," I said.

"You'll see us at the next mile marker. Now get going!" Mom again. I smiled, nodded, jumped up and down for good measure, and started running, again.

A peculiar thing happens when you find a good rhythm with running. You sync up with the beating of your own heart and all the outside noise of the world falls away, blends in with the rushing of your blood. I don't actually know that any of this is true, I read it in a magazine, but is sure sounds good. The actual truth of what running felt like was closer to agony, with a chaser of intense pain.

I looked at my watch.

I'd been running for seven minutes. How far was a mile? And how many did I have left?

Ugh.

Stupid. Stupid. Thud thud thud.

What was that thudding?

Was that my actual heart beating or my feet against the concrete?

It was neither. It was Megan pushing herself next to me in the wheel chair, cradling mom in her lap. "Didn't we say we'd be with you the whole way?" Megan asked.

"It's an excellent time to play therapist," Mom offered.

"Can't. Talk. Dying. Here," I panted.

"Oh, good, dear. I wasn't really talking about you anyway. I've had another dream about Matt Damon . . ."

40

The Run
Continued
Dear God Will This Insanity Ever Stop???

While Mom talked about some dream involving an intricate chocolate mousse recipe and meditating in Hawaii, I did a peculiar thing. I ran. I just ran. I stopped thinking. I just ran. My mom's voice became a weird, comforting hum, along with the wheels of Megan's wheelchair going round and round, and I somehow slipped inside my own body and I just . . . was. I passed mile 2, mile 3, mile 5 and 6, and I was doing fine.

At mile 7, I threw up. But that was just a set back.

At mile 7.1 I stumbled.

At mile 7.15 I gave up.

"Aw, fuck it! Just fucking fuck it. Fuck the fucker fuckelo-fuck."

"Tell us how you really feel," Megan said. She scratched her turtle head. It had enormous eyes that were just staring at me and looking, I swear, very disappointed. "Chloe, just shut up will you?" her little turtle mouth said.

What? What! "Shut up?" I said. Or, okay, I screamed. I said really loudly while runners huffed and puffed past me. "You want me to shut up! I'm the one running here! Me. And I'm tired. This is pathetic. And stupid. Why did I say I was going to do this? What's the point? What's the point of any of this really? Matt is just a fucking fantasy and I've become this pathetic crybaby, crying over a man I've only kissed once, maybe twice, or three times or what-fuck-ever, a man who just thinks of me as a friend."

"That's the saddest story I've ever heard," said a voice behind me. I turned and it was the bald groping guy. "Sort of makes me want to stop running too."

"Go away!" I snapped. The guy ran off.

I started crying then. I'm not proud of this, but that's why this is called a confession. I'm not saying this was easy or that I won the stupid race. No. I'm saying I had a breakdown on the shore of Lake Michigan and I sobbed at my mother's turtle feet, while Megan stroked my hair with her turtle fins.

After a moment, Mom patted my back and then said: "Okay, Chloe, dear. You've had enough."

I looked up at her, relieved that I could just give up, stop, and we could go home.

"You've got just about 6 miles to go, and then we'll call it a night," she finished.

I looked at her, disbelieving.

"Go. Run. You said you were going to do this, and we're here to make sure you do, because sometimes you have to do incredibly stupid things to . . ." she paused here and then went silent.

"Jesus, Mom, a little more insight here. Why do I have to do incredibly stupid things?"

"Because that's called living, dear. Later, you learn from it. Right now, you just suffer."

Just suffer.

Just suffer through it.

Now there's something I could connect with. If there was anything in the world I was good at, it was suffering. I put one foot in front of the other, and then I was running again.

***

I thought about a lot of things on those 6 miles of running. I thought I'd die. (I didn't.) I thought I couldn't possibly do it. (I could.) I thought about Megan and Mom wheeling alongside me telling me they loved me, believed in me, wanted me to accomplish this, all while enclosed in gigantic turtle costumes. And I realized as I ran, that I wasn't running for Matt anymore. Or to show Amber something. And I sort of wasn't even running for myself. I was running for my family: for Megan and my mom because they loved me and I wanted them to be proud. And so I ran.

From the outside, if you were a spectator, you wouldn't even think I was running. It looked more like walking with wild arm swinging, but inside, like internally, I was that god with the wings on his feet, Apollo or Nike or something like that. I was on fire.

And when the finish line loomed in front of me, I couldn't believe it. It was a mirage, surely. But it wasn't. I saw it. Mom and Megan were going ballistic. And there, right at the end of the line, was Matt, looking me right in the eyes, staring at me, at me, running, and not even noticing Amber next to him.

And when I crossed the finish line, first I hugged my

mom and Megan, and then I went over to Matt and I did the most natural thing in the world: I slugged him.

I regret that action and the actions that follow, not only because they landed me in jail overnight, but because I also broke a nail.

41

Me, Channeling Rocky

"Ugh," Matt cried, or something equally barbaric-sounding. I'd meant to knock him on the nose and cause a volcanic gusher, but he's so much taller than me that I ended up hitting him in the throat. Right in the Adam's apple. God. I could've killed him or something. Who knew I was so fierce?

"That's for leading me on," I said. He grunted again. He was sort of turning purple. "Oh, God, are you okay? I didn't mean to kill you, I just meant to . . ."

"Teach me a lesson?" he wheezed. I nodded. "I got it," he said. And then he smiled at me! The fucker smiled at me!!

He was so confusing.

I wanted to kiss him.

And then I did kiss him. Again. What was up with me and kissing this poor man? Why couldn't I stop it? Why couldn't I . . . oh . . . kisskisskiss . . . because kissing him felt good. Incredibly good. He wrapped his big bear arms around me, and I fit in next to him the way a pretzel from the mall loops in on itself. And his tongue! I know tongues don't sound sexy, and it may even sound a bit gross, but it wasn't just me kissing him, it was him kissing me, or rather his tongue opening my mouth ever so gently and his hands were down my back and in my hair and OH GOD what was that swelling I felt with our two bodies pressed . . .

"MOTHERFUCKER!!!!!" screamed Amber. And then she was on me, pulling me away from Matt, and then instead of rolling on the ground with Matt, I was rolling on the ground with Amber and we were swearing and hissing and tufts of hair were wafting up into the cool night air and we knocked into some runners and heard a scream . . . and it wasn't my fault the lady broke her hip. She was ninety-five years old. What was she doing running a half marathon anyway? It wasn't my fault. "It's not my fault!" I cried as Chad and a police officer pulled us apart.

I kept screaming too as they picked me up and tossed me in the only police car on the island. It wasn't a police car at all, but a police carriage, and there I was staring at a horse's butt again.

By that I mean, of course, Amber. They threw her in next to me and I stared at her. Oh, I stared at her long and hard.

Take that, bitch.

42

The Blues, Out Of Key And Oh-So-Bad

"Oh, I'm so low I could cry, I'm so low I could die, I'm so low I don't know why, I'm really hungry for apple pie . . ." I was sitting in Mackinac Island's 100% realistic barracks, singing the blues. Or what I could remember of the blues. Since I couldn't remember any blues at all, I was just sort of making up my own lyrics. Mostly I sang because it felt good to sing, and poetic somehow, but I could also tell that my voice was driving Amber batty. *"I'm so low I'm a fly . . ."*

"You certainly are," said Amber and then she glared at me with her laser beam eyes.

"Did you say something or did a cockroach burp?" I asked the air.

"Yeah. Yeah. I did say something. And I'm saying something now."

"Oh, yeah?" I was exhausted. My legs were pudding, my brown socks were falling down, my U.P. Yours t-short had stains on it, and I had the bald guy's phone number in my bra. I was itching for a fight. "What exactly are you saying?"

"I'm saying something." Amber said, very seriously. "Listen." She paused and cocked her head. "Something. See?"

"Wow. Well, that something is pretty fierce."

"Yeah. It is." She looked at me.

"Yeah?" I looked at her.

"Yeah."

We were in a stare-down. Suddenly there was a weird tin whistle, of the spaghetti western variety. Just me and Amber, staring each other down in a turn of the century barracks.

I don't know who started laughing first, but I'm pretty sure it wasn't me.

"Oh my God," she breathed. "This is just pathetic."

"I know. It really is." I bent to pick a piece of grass out of my shoe. Or was it hair? Please, please don't be hair. It wasn't. I'm not sure what it was . . .

"Look, Chloe, it's really cold and I'm exhausted and I'm supposed to get married tomorrow and I just . . ." (I'd really forgotten they'd come up here to elope. I'd forgotten they were supposed to get married at all. It was rather shocking to be reminded of it.) Amber seemed to be having trouble breathing.

"You okay?" I asked. I really was concerned.

She shook her head and took a humongous breath, the way a sea monster might sound before blowing out its blowhole or something. "I just . . ." She really wasn't breathing very well. "I . . ."

And then she was crying, and not dainty tears either; these were Man Tears and great gasping sobs. What else could I do? I took the poor girl in my arms and patted her bird-like back.

Karma better be paying attention.

***

Seventy-five minutes later . . .

"God, how embarrassing," Amber breathed.

She was sitting in front of me, cross-legged on the cold barracks floor and I was doing weird twisty things with her hair. I had no hair talent at all (that's why I keep mine short) but I discovered I could make fantastic sculptures by tying little knots and sort of fraying the hair. Right now, I was creating an ice skating scene with Amber's hair, and it looked like one of the skaters had fallen into the ice. Ah well. No one could see us anyway, which was probably a good thing. All of Amber's makeup had slid from her eyes in great dark stripes down her cheeks, and met at her neck. It was sort of like she was wearing an Egyptian necklace, only it started on her face. Her eyes and nose were red and puffy, and there was grass and dirt stuck all over her. And she smelled. Bad.

I didn't look much better. She'd just done my hair.

And we'd traded shirts.

"I don't know what I'm doing here." She said softly.

"We got into a fight," I reminded her.

"You kicked my ass." She blew her nose onto her (my) shirt.

"I would've if they hadn't stopped me."

"Yeah," she said. "Maybe I needed it."

I didn't know how to answer that, and then she continued, saving me from saying something awkward and misplaced. "I didn't mean how I got *here*, in jail, but how I got here at *all*."

"Mackinac Island? Turtle Race?"

"No. Matt."

His name kind of just hung out there, floating in front of us like an unwanted ghost. I felt my throat constrict, the way it does when you bite into a lemon, or you're about to cry uncontrollably. To stop myself from crying, I thought about how Amber was feeling about all of this. I mean, imagine, the love of your life, the guy you're engaged to, invites you to a romantic getaway in Northern Michigan where you're going to run away together (literally) and then get married, and then some crazy chick shows up with her mom and an equally crazy woman in a wheel chair, and suddenly your fiancé is making out with her, and your heart is just broken.

Your heart is broken.

Her heart was broken.

Amber's heart was broken.

My heart was just bent. I mean, Matt and I had just kissed a couple of times, had no commitment, and most of our relationship existed only in my head. "Amber . . ." I said tentatively. My throat was still tight. "I'm really . . ." Oh shoot. I was crying. God damn you, estrogen!! "I'm really sorry."

She turned to look at me. I almost laughed at her crazy hair and makeup. "What on earth are *you* sorry about?"

"I'm sorry I came up here. I'm sorry about . . . about Matt . . . about my behavior. I'm going to leave you both alone. You'll never see me again. That is, if they ever let us out of here."

Amber opened her mouth to speak, but I'm not sure what she was going to say. I was too busy staring at the two giant turtles saying "Psssst!!! PSSSSST! CHLOEEEEEE!"

43

The Incredibly Exciting Prison Break!
Or
Opening The Door And Walking Out

"Mom? Megan? Chad? What are you guys doing here?"

Mom held out an ancient ring of keys. "We are busting you out of here."

"You're what?"

"Busting you out," said Mom, smiling. "It's a good old-fashioned breakout."

"Jailbreak," Megan corrected.

"Well," Chad said, taking the key from mom and unlocking the cell. "It's not really a jailbreak. I know the guy who's in charge here. Buddy. He has a bar bill about a foot long. So he owes me."

Amber and I stood up, and we both started adjusting ourselves in a suspicious way: you know, pulling our shirts down, smoothing our hair, not looking each other in the eyes, stuff like that.. "Were you guys making out or something?" asked Megan.

"No. No! Why?"

"Because you look incredibly guilty." She eyed me warily.

Chad swung the door open.

"We were just *talking*," I said.

"Really?" Mom and Megan asked at the same time.

I walked out of the cell. Freedom felt good. The way it felt to go without underwear sometimes. Liberating. Fresh. "Yes. Really." Megan spun herself around in her rented wheelchair and we all started walking down the hallway. Buddy waved to us. Some jailbreak. That's when I noticed Amber wasn't with us. "Wait a minute," I said. "I forgot something."

I ran back to the cell and she was sitting on the floor, a deflated balloon, biting on her nails. "Amber?"

She looked up at me, and her blue eyes sparked. "Yeah?" The word was all soft and hopeful, and, man was I feeling like a real asshole.

"You coming with us?"

I swear it was like she'd just received an invitation from Jesus himself. She was beaming. "Oh, yeah! Yeah, sure. I'd love to!" She bounced up and ran for the door.

We walked silently down the hallway together.

Buddy told us to have a good night.

We nodded.

Just before we reached Mom, Megan and Chad, Amber put her hand on my shoulder. "Why are they dressed like ogres?"

"Ogres? No. No! They're dressed like *turtles*." I said.

"Oh. Okay," she said, as if that explained everything.

She really wasn't half bad, that Amber.

44

Reality
The Reason They Invented Antidepressants

It was dark out. Quiet dark. The kind of dark where you could just feel people in their beds breathing, dreaming of puppies or orgasms . . . but hopefully not puppies having orgasms because that's just plain weird. "Sheesh. How long were we in there?" I asked, looking up at the dark sky dotted with stars.

Chad checked his watch and pushed a little indiglo button. "About six hours. Give or take."

"Give or take what?"

"A second."

"Okay . . ." I said and then took a look at Megan. Chad was pretty precise. Come to think of it, he was downright perfect: every hair in place, extremely organized, and smelling of soap. And he knew how long we'd been in captivity down to the second. I'm sure Megan was rolling her eyes about that. His attention to time was a sure sign of uptightedness, and Megan hated uptightedness. I could almost feel the annoyance pouring after her. I'm not sure her relationship with Chad would survive this vacation, because it didn't seem to survive sobriety. And just as I was thinking this he leaned down and whispered to her and she giggled. Megan actually giggled.

I really should stop analyzing other people. I always got them wrong.

And if I always got other people wrong, maybe I was getting myself wrong . . . maybe I was . . .

I didn't know. I was too wiped out to think. I concentrated on sensory details instead, like my stomach growling for food, the smell of the lake, the rush of the waves pushing and pulling against the shore, the throbbing of my legs — legs that had survived 13.1 miles and were still going strong. You get the picture.

I soaked things in. I listened. The five of us sounded like horses clomping down the brick paved hill.

And then I saw that there really were horses clomping down the brick paved hill. They were just in front of us. At the bottom of the hill, they came to a stop, and a dark figure jumped out of the carriage. I couldn't see any of the man's features, he was just a dark shape against the blue lake rolling behind him, but I knew who it was. There was only one man who made my heart go arrhythmic: Matt. Beautiful Matt. Funny Matt. Sexy Matt. My Mmmmmm. Who was not my Mmmmmm. But was Amber's.

And as we walked closer I saw that he held something in his hands. A bouquet of flowers.

Amber squeezed my shoulder again. "I guess I better go," she said.

"Okay," I said.

"Do you want to see us off? Say something to him? I mean, it must be . . ."

"Hard. Yeah. No. You go ahead. You both go ahead. And be happy together, okay? Really. Just . . . I don't know . . . be happy."

She smiled and gave me a hug. "You too," she said. And then she bounded off.

I couldn't bear to watch. I didn't have to.

"Uhm, Chloe . . . Megan and your mom thought, that is . . . I suggested . . . well . . ." Chad was clearly at a loss.

"We have a getaway boat," Megan finished. "If you want it. We can escape into the moonlight and he'll never know where we've gone."

Escape sounded pretty delicious.

"Fred McClusiac, the guy who owns the ferry has a bar bill . . ." Chad began.

"A foot long?" I asked.

"Yeah." He smiled. "And he owes me a favor."

"You're using a lot of your favors up this weekend," I said trying to sound all happy when all I felt was misery.

"Yeah, well, it's worth it." He looked pointedly at Megan.

I turned my head and saw something I truly didn't expect: Megan was smiling. I hadn't seen her smile that way in years, not even with Eric.

"All right, troops, let's head out!" Mom called and marched us in the direction of our getaway.

I didn't turn to watch Amber and Matt go.

I didn't have to.

I could hear the sound of their carriage echoing off the road before them, even when I was sitting in the boat, waves splashing against the hull, moonlight pouring over us, I could still the hollow sound of their horses receding.

Part Three

45

Me,
Or Should I Say Moi,
A Tormented Movie Star

If my life were a French film, it would've ended with that episode. Picture: Me in a boat, tears streaming down my face, and then I'd look at the camera and in a voice over you'd hear something really deep, something like "The loss of my lake is blue". And then the credits would roll, and you'd walk out of the theatre pretending you understood what the hell just happened.

Jesus.

Maybe my life *was* a French film after all because for four hot sweaty summer months, I'd been telling myself that everything (i.e. my nonrelationship with Matt) made perfect sense and I understood perfectly what had happened up north (he didn't love me) and there was nothing wrong with me at all (I was not a loser). "The loss of my lake is blue" sort of made sense. Yep. Yep. Uh-huh.

Oh god. Oh god!!! It was all bunk. I didn't understand anything, least of all why I kept having lip-smacking fantasies about a man who was married to a non-she-devil.

Truth was, I was as big of a mess as ever, only I had a permasmile on to cover it up.

I'd convinced myself that I'd gotten my life together. I was working steadily at Bud & Julie's Bistro, had a good line on a full time job at Grand Rapids Music Center, and Megan was still my roommate with occasional weekend absences when she traveled up north (sans cast) to visit a certain first kisser of mine. Mom was settled in at the retirement village and had started teaching other retirees how to connect with their spirituality, sexuality and sentimentality. What that meant was she taught classes on how to practice the Kama Sutra either with a partner or on your own. Life was going just fine. I'd even gone out on a date with someone.

And then I saw him.

At Monster Burrito.

And good golly, there is a reason I refer to myself as Blunder Woman. I just get sucked into the vortex every time. But this happened later, first, the getting myself together part, then seeing Matt again, and again, then, the final blunder. The worst blunder of all time. The real doozy. Committed not by me this time, but by Matt himself.

Ugh.

46

An Offer I Couldn't Refuse
And It Wasn't Sexual

Just four short months after the Race of the Turtles, (and when I say short months, I mean the longest months of my life) and I was doing just great. Why, I wasn't thinking about Matt at all. Not his lips, or his voice, or how our children would look, or what he would look like naked when he was trying to give me children, or what kind of positions I'd try with him while we weren't thinking about children at all but just focused on having amazing toe curling sex.

What was I saying?

Oh. Yes.

I wasn't thinking about Matt at all.

And I certainly wasn't thinking about him while I was trying to come up with a fundraiser that would make Classical music funny. Lisa, the Executive Director of the Grand Rapids Music Center, liked my grant writing skills. We'd had coffee a number of times and had that peculiar connection that sometimes happens where you knew you'd be friends with someone if they weren't your boss and you were scared to death they wouldn't hire you again. I liked her. She was about ten years older than me and really put together, meaning, she'd completed her therapy and was now successfully managing life on her own. She was also a quirky genius, with crazy curly hair like mine and this smile that was all teeth and gleam, and so when she called me out of the blue and said with her characteristically truncated style: "Chloe. Super idea. My office. Twelve. Bring chocolate." I was there. Interested, intrigued and entirely a basket case. Was she going to fire me? Would she tell me the last grant I'd emailed from Mackinac Island was riddled with some guy called "Matt" and had nothing to do with raising funds for her organization?

But no. That wasn't what happened at all.

I sat in her office in a big creaky leather chair. She looked at me, winked, shut the door and then clicked on her favorite 80's radio station online. "Sometimes classical music puts me right to sleep," she said.

"At least it makes your brain bigger," I offered.

"Just what I need, a bigger brain." She knocked on her head with her knuckles, and I actually heard her brain sigh. She was, honestly, one of the most brilliant people I'd ever met. "No. What I need is a bigger bank account for our kids' programs. And that's where you come in." She pointed me. Even though I was the only one in the office, I still looked behind me to see if she were referring to someone else. Lisa shook her head, laughing. "I'm talking to you, Chloe. Chloe Knaggs. Grant writer extraordinaire."

I was starting to feel a little uncomfortable. Had I slipped into an alternate universe and not yet realized it?

Lisa continued, leaning in to talk excitedly. "I know your background is in grant writing, but I think you have the right personality for this. We need an event that can raise us $16,000 or I have to shut down the facility." She said this with a perkiness that belied the seriousness of what she was saying. "Okay. Maybe not the entire facility. That's a little severe, but I will need to close the kids' programs. And it's depressing as all get out. I need some fresh ideas here. We've tried committees and subcommittees, and I just can't hold another auction or musical event or ladies tea. I need something different. And you, my dear, are different. You don't say classical music at all when I look at you."

"Do I say Laurence Welk when you look at me?" I liked Laurence Welk, a little guilty secret of mine, and I was afraid it showed.

Lisa laughed. "Goodness, no. You say: Something Different."

"Whew. That's a relief."

Lisa nodded. "Very good. We agree. What I'm struggling with here, is that this musical society is still stuck in the 1800's and I need something modern. Something now. Something that can make people pry open their rusty little wallets and give our organization some money. And what with the economy and this being Michigan . . ." She made a gesture that I took to mean: blah blah blah. "I need an *event*. And not just any event. It's got to be something that informs our community about what we do, how we support and encourage musicians, how classical music can shape and form minds and most importantly, it's got to be fun. Funny. You know, something people will actually want to attend. Know what

I mean?"

I nodded even though inside I was curled up like a shrimp.

Classical music=funny. A real laugh riot.

"All right then. Go!" She spun around in her chair and started typing at her computer. "That means get started. I need a list of ideas from you in three hours. And if you get this right . . ." she turned around and faced me. "I'll offer you a part-time job. And the future? Who knows. Maybe health insurance." She paused dramatically. "And dental."

I think I orgasmed right there.

After an adulthood of praying not to get sick and not exactly knowing where my next paying gig was coming from or if it was coming at all, Lisa was offering me my heart's desire: stability. Or, at least, one of my heart's desires: stability in a job. I still had an unanswered heart's desire lurking in the background . . . but I was not thinking about him. Or his lips. Or his sexy clavicles. Mmmmm.

Lisa and I stood up, high-fived, did a complicated handshake with lots of tricky hand moves, and I did the Hustle out of there.

Wait. Scratch that. That was only a musical montage in my head. A side-effect of being raised by the television.

No. I just ran out of the office, to The Beast (whish I'd borrowed) and started making a list of possible themes.

I only thought about Matt twice. (If you mean twice as in two hundred times, like twice a hundred. Then I only thought of him twice.)

And in the end, I came up with an idea. A stupid, brilliant, shiny, self-destructive idea that could only happen if I contacted Matt again.

Ugh. What's that word again? Oh yeah. Masochistic. That's me. I should probably have my mom write a t-shirt with that on it.

47

Me

Currently

Again With Megan

(And you know what I mean by that)

An hour later, I was sitting comfortably with Megan in our favorite place on the planet: Bud & Julie's Bistro, the place where I sometimes waited tables if they were really busy, but mostly just wasted time. Megan and I were chomping along while I wrote things on a list, and then aggressively crossed them out. I sort of looked a bit like Mozart composing, what with his crazy hair and everything. Or was that Beethoven? Not the deaf one. The other one.

Oh, forget it.

At any rate, if you hadn't guessed, Megan was getting along just fine. Limping a little, sure, but no cast anymore. She was now my official roommate. I had her rent check to prove it. She said I forced her into it. I said "Bribery isn't a sign of force; it's a sign of affection." I told her I wanted her to move in so badly, that if she didn't I'd tell everyone on Facebook about her Donny & Marie collection. Instant presto roommate. Easy. She had a sometime visitor come and stay with her, namely, Chad, but she never wanted to talk about that. If I even breathed the word 'relationship' to her, she was liable to go all X-Men Phoenix on me and burn me to ashes.

I scratched another idea off the list.

Megan worked on the last bite of one of Julie's amazing pulled BBQ beef sandwiches. Her sandwiches were so amazing we weren't sure if they're really meat. Meat didn't taste that good. No, it must've been Soylent Green instead. Julie came out of the kitchen balancing her little girl Janeway on her hip. "Lunch was busy today," she said.

"It was rocking," I said. "Are you sure you don't want to stay open for dinners too? I'm sure this place would be packed. You could probably double your income."

Julie smiled. "Yeah," she said. "I could. But there are more important things than income right now."

Janeway made a burbling sound. "I farted!" she screamed happily.

"Good for you," Megan said in a way that sounded as if she was very impressed.

"Are you sure you don't want something else to eat?" Julie asked gently. I was working on a half-eaten cup of soup. It was my favorite: a velvety lobster bisque, but my brain was too focused on the task on hand to focus on getting soup successfully into my mouth. I looked up at her and shook my head. I swear to God Julie was a mother-goddess herself. How was it possible to be a great cook, a super mom, have a cute as hell husband, and your own business to boot? Plus there was her fabulous friend (on vacation in Canada somewhere with her beefcake husband and twin boys.) It just didn't seem right. Some people just have it easy, I guess.

"Maybe I'll have cake later," I said. "But first I've got to finish this." I held up my list. It looked like a deranged child's letter to Santa. I really should have found something else to write with besides a red crayon.

Julie nodded. "Then why don't you and Megan wait a second? I'll make you a little dessert. You don't have to be hungry for it. Dessert has nothing to do with hunger. Come on Janeway."

Janeway followed Julie to the kitchen then turned and I swear she flashed the Vulcan sign with her little fingers. Her parents were way into sci-fi. It was the cutest thing I've ever seen.

I looked at Megan and sighed. It was a sigh of longing, I must say, because that empty space in my heart and head, the place Matt used to reside, was still wide open. "I'm going to give up sex," I said.

Megan finished her last bite. "I thought you already did. Ages ago."

"Yeah, but that wasn't by choice. That was by circumstance. Now I'm just giving it up."

"Tell me if Matt walked in that door right now you wouldn't throw yourself at his feet and have sex with him."

"On the floor? In front of people? Ick. I'd take him in the back room at least." I sighed again. It was that kind of day.

"Stop thinking about him. Work on your fundraising idea."

"I'm trying to work on an idea and I just can't come up

with anything. Every idea I have is exactly like every other fundraiser out there. Silent Auction. Live Auction. Live auction where everyone is silent. Bingo. Gambling. Musical Theatre Revue. It's all tired exhausting stuff, and none of it says that classical music is fun. And I wouldn't pay a penny for any of it."

"That was nice," Megan said.

"What was?"

"For thirty seconds there, you lifted your head out of Pathetic Land."

"Thank you." And then I raised my head a little higher. "I fucking just had an epiphany."

Julie came out of the kitchen just then carrying a white plate with a mound of chocolate cake. She set it in front of me. "Holy mother of God . . ." I whispered. "Is that . . ."

She nodded. "The Vulcan Volcano. Enjoy."

"I love you," I said.

"I know."

48

"Christmas Story" Got It Right.
Never Succumb To A Triple Dog Dare.

The Vulcan Volcano was a sinful creation of dark chocolate cake with a luscious lava chocolate center surrounded by crème anglaise and topped with a single chocolate covered cherry that looked like a crater. I haven't the words to describe. It's beyond amazing, and the timing of it at that particular moment, couldn't have been better. I needed something to slap my creative juices going, and a disco with sugar was just the ticket. Megan and I dug in. I may not have been hungry, but I wasn't stupid either.

"I could give up sex for a year too," Megan said when we're finished. "Especially after that. I swear I just had an orgasm."

"Just now?"

"Right now. I'm orgasming right now."

"Wow."

"Don't tell Chad."

We laughed and then Megan looked at me with that

scary twinkle in her eye. "I dare you," she said and pointed with her chocolate tipped fork to the guy by the window bobbing his head. We'd seen him there countless times before, and I could never figure out if he were listening to music or just twitching occasionally. He had that dark-haired poet-wannabe look: messy locks covering his eyes, always carrying a book and writing poems into. At least I hoped they were poems and not, like, vendettas.

"You dare me to what?" I asked, though I didn't really have to. I knew exactly what she was thinking. She wanted me to talk to that guy in the hopes that Matt could get shoved out of my heart.

"I dare you to . . . ask that dude out. It's time."

"No it isn't."

"You're right. It's past time. Annoyingly past time. You've got to move on."

"You sound like my mom."

"Your mom is a smart lady."

"You're just quoting one of her t-shirts."

Megan set her fork down on the table and shot me A Look. This one said "You Better Do This For Me Because I'm Your Roommate and You're Driving Me Insane."

"I have never responded to a dare," I said stubbornly.

She pointed her fork at him.

"Except this once," I said, and I tossed my napkin on the table the way I imagined one would throw down the gauntlet.

49

Take That, Megan.

"Excuse me," I said to the guy in the corner swaying to some music or suffering from Toerrets. He looked up at me and the first thing I noticed were his eyes. Hello, Blue. Like bright blue, sparkling. Matt had brown eyes. I'd always liked brown eyes, but *blue*. Hmmm.

And then he gave me a little half-smile. "Hey," he said. We nodded to each other.

I looked at Megan so that she noticed I was about to prove a point. I squared my shoulders. "Listen, I won't have sex with you, but would you like to go out tonight? I thought we could go listen to jazz somewhere, order a cocktail, talk, you know." I don't say anything about un-coffee because, well, been there, done that.

"Jazz, cocktail, but no sex?" he asked. His voice was low, a bit husky or breathy, and made me tilt in a little more to hear him. He had, yes, a Vampire Voice. Lovely. And there was that little half-smile again.

"Yeah. Exactly. No sex tonight or tomorrow or probably forever, really. At least for a year anyway. I've given it up."

"But jazz is okay with you?"

"Sure. Jazz is great."

"Okay," he said. He popped his earplugs back in. "I dig jazz." Then he bobbed his head to the music, flipped the page in his book and I turned and gave Megan the thumbs up. That was god-awful easy. I pulled the napkin from under his plate, grabbed my pen and wrote "The BOB, 8pm, My name's Chloe" on it. He read it, gave me the thumbs up back and then returned to his book. I tried to peak to see if he were writing manifestos or just bad poetry, but I couldn't see anything except some pen marks.

I walked back to the table with Megan and I was smiling. I just asked a guy out. Not on a date, really, but I asked a non-Matt guy to spend time with me. I wondered if I could've asked him out if sex were still on the table (or the floor, or in front of a fire place). Probably not. It was sort of freeing asking someone out and just being totally clear about what you wanted. The way I should've been with Matt. I should never have asked Matt out for un-coffee. I should have asked him out on a relationship. But this was good. This was progress. And since I really had committed to no sex for a year, I could relax knowing there was no pressure, it wasn't going to happen, not for 365 days, and not with this guy. No. It was going to happen with Matt. Why? Because I was sure I was psychic. At least when I wanted to be.

I sat back down at the table looking smug and pleased with myself.

"Get back to work," Megan said. "You need to focus."

"Right," I said. Focus focus focus. On fundraising.

Making classical music fun. Raising money. Something quirky. Some kind of party that wasn't indoors, in a concert hall, but out in the fresh air. And that's when I got the idea. And honestly, Matt wasn't connected with it at all, except it was where I met him, where he presumably still worked, where he and me and St. Cecilia had originally crossed paths: The Westwood Career Development Center aka The Happy Place. I was going to throw a huge fundraiser at a ropes course . . . Matt M. be damned.

Of course, I'd need his help, but I was feeling too puffed up with myself to think on that at the moment (or maybe it was just denial or some other therapy term).

"I've got an idea," I said to Megan. "A serious idea."

"It's about time," she said. "Lay it on me."

50

One For Me

"No," Megan said.

"But . . ."

"No. No! You know why?"

"Why?" I asked.

"Because you're stupid."

"Megan! You can't call your roommate and best friend stupid. That's not nice."

"And it's not nice to put yourself or Matt or his wife or *me* through it either."

She had a point there.

"But it's a really good idea," I said, starting to feel a little less convinced than I had when I'd started. "It has to be The Happy Place, which is, uhm, Matt's Happy Place. I don't know of any other ropes courses here. And it's quirky and fun and just weird enough that people might show up. And Matt owes me, dammit. He *owes* me. Where else could I get a venue for free? It's for the kids, Megan. And their little classically undeveloped brains."

She harrumphed. She really did. She might as well have

said "Bah Humbug," but she just harrumphed instead. And then she said: "You better be careful. I'll be watching you." She pointed two fingers at me as if she were issuing a curse.

"I know," I said. "I am always careful."

"You are not."

"I know," I admitted. I contemplated licking the last of the chocolate sauce off my plate, and then said, fuck it, leaned over , and did it.

"You have no shame," said Megan.

"I know again."

"I'm glad you did that, because now I can too." And we both licked our plates clean. Literally.

It isn't an uncommon site at Bud & Julie's, really. People do it all the time.

Feeling sated, I picked up my red crayon and began writing like a maniac. My phone rang and it was Lisa. "Last minute change of plans," she said. "I've got to go out in five minutes with a potential donor so I have to cancel our meeting. I want to see you bright and early tomorrow and you can pitch me your genius."

We said our goodbyes, hung up, and I exhaled deeply. It gave me twelve hours or so to work out the kinks in the idea. I exhaled again.

"Practicing your yoga at long last?" Megan asked.

"No, just relief." And just as I was starting to feel relaxed for the first time in weeks, the guy with the cute-poet hair walked over, knocked on the table and said, "See you tonight."

We watched him leave.

"Ach," I breathed.

"You'd already forgotten, hadn't you?"

I had. It was easy to forget. I didn't really mean to make a date with the guy, I just meant to make Megan laugh.

"And before you relax too much, your mom is due at the apartment in half an hour."

I'd forgotten that too. It was Tuesday, the night Mom came over bearing Chex Mix and 1950's movies and she practiced Reiki or perms or manicures on us.

Shit. Shit shit shit. Shit. Shit-shit-shit-shit.

Really.

My brain was already pounding.

The good news though, with all the work brainstorming, Vulcan licking, pseudo-flirting, and impending mom-dom, I didn't have any time to think about Matt at all. In fact, I had another twelve hours while I created and textured my fundraising plan and wouldn't have to think about him again until, well, at least the morning.

Take that, Mmm. One for me. Nothing for him.

51

When You're Depressed, I Guess You Really Do Look Like Those Losers In Drug Ads

Really, I couldn't eat more or I'd have to wear a sweatsuit. After Bud & Julie's, Megan and I came home to an apartment smelling of caramelized butter and garlic. It was the damned Chex Mix. A simple cereal recipe, but I swear to god, it was like my mom massaged the cereal or something. It was so garlicky and crunchy that you couldn't kiss anyone for days after eating it, not that I was planning on kissing anyone anyway.

After the food coma set in, the three of us focused on our own thing: Megan was on the couch playing an Agatha Christie video game. Those games were so intensely boring; I didn't know how she did it. She'd spend hours just lifting up animated coffee cups trying to figure out stuff when she could just flip open a real book and the answer was all there. Mom was flipping tarot cards out onto the coffee table in what looked like some rainbow design. And I was busy not getting ready for my date.

How could I put effort into something I'd asked for as

a joke, an afterthought? It was easier to just eat Chex Mix. It certainly didn't feel like I was going on a date. It felt more like an appointment. For a pap smear.

"You've got to at least shower," said my mom.

"Why should I shower? It's not like I'm seeing Matt."

"Maybe he's not Matt, sure. But he is a person. The cards clearly say you should shower."

"Do they really?"

"No. I do," Mom said. "You, my sweet girl, stink."

"I stink?"

"Bad," concurred Megan. "You smell like mushrooms."

I sniffed myself as I schlepped to the bathroom. Did I smell like mushrooms? And weren't mushrooms some sort of a fungus? Did I smell like a fungus? That was deeply disturbing. It occurred to me then that I couldn't remember the last time I'd showered, or brushed my hair, or, Buddha in nirvana, when I'd shaved. I could shave secret codes into the amount of hair I had on my legs. And between my thighs. And . . . do we really need to go there?

Maybe I was depressed.

I sat on the toilet.

"You're depressed!" My mom called to me. "The cards say so. You've got swords piercing hearts all over the place! You've either got to have fun tonight or I'm putting you in therapy for real."

I waited for a beat and then I heard Megan yell "Ditto!"

They were freaking me out.

Though I do have to say, the shower felt miraculous: just hot enough to relax, not hot enough to hurt. Which is exactly what I needed in a mate.

Ho-hum.

I wished there was a TV show that made depression sexy the way they'd made anorexia oh-so-trendy. Why couldn't I, for once, be trendy instead of just sad and frumpy?

52

Another Example Of My Weirdness Magnet

Five minutes later, I was clean, smelling of ginger and orange (so the soap label said), and fifteen minutes later, I was in The Beast on my way to The BOB, or The Big Old Building, but The BOB is a lot catchier. It's a series of restaurants built into what used to be some kind of furniture warehouse and managed to not really be cool at all. But they had a jazz bar that I liked and lots of people to get lost among if I needed to make a quick exit. So. There I was headed. I'd left Mom and Megan to read each other's tealeaves or something equally strange. I've found it's better not to ask exactly what they do when they hang out.

When I walked into the Blue Note, I saw he was already waiting for me, his head bob bob bobbing along. And there wasn't even any music playing.

I could have turned away right then. I could have turned and ran, but I was wearing heels and I never wear heels and I was so wobbly and if I stepped on something wrong or hit a wet spot on the floor . . . I'd go flying. I started to envision all the crazy things that could happen to me when I realized my date was waving at me like a madman batting a swarm of locusts: meaning he was waving with both hands in a crazy windmill pattern . . . and there were no locusts.

There was no use running. I'd been spotted. So I waggle wobbled over to him, hoping I looked sexy and not like one leg was shorter than the other. (One leg is, but it's hardly noticeable.) I didn't particularly want to look sexy for him, I didn't even know him, but every woman can relate to wanting to look sexy in general. It's just this unwritten urge that all the advertisers know about: we want to feel like everyone in a room gasps when we enter. I heard at least one gasp, but it might have been more of a burp. They were doing wine tastings at the bar.

I plopped down. Really. I made a little plop sound when I sat. It was a little disturbing. Well. There. He, at least, was staring at me. Just . . . staring. Staring for a really long time and not saying anything at all. "Uhm, hello?" I offered.

"You don't remember me do you?"

"I just met you a few hours ago. Of course I remember you."

"Oh, sure, yeah, but no. I mean, you don't remember me from . . . before." It was the way he said 'before' that made my heart stop, of — what is that expression guys use when they're terrified — like their balls have curled up inside them. I'm sure I was feeling exactly that. My little phantom balls curling up inside me.

I didn't remember any Before. But it was possible. I was terrible at remembering people. It was sort of like even when I was talking to someone, my mind could be universes away and I could have entire conversations and not remember the person I had the conversation with at all. Sort of what I was doing at that moment. Instead of talking to him, I was staring off into the distance. When I snapped to, he was still looking at me, all expectantly, like a dog looking dreamily at the can opener and all it can offer to them.

Shit! Shit. Before. What Before? What was I supposed to say? Did I have sex with him? What if I had sex with him! I've never forgotten having sex with someone. Have I? I'd remember having sex with him. But if you don't remember then you wouldn't know you didn't have sex with him. Or did. Fuck, I was confused. So I said: "No."

"I'm Evan. Evan Young? 6th Grade? Mrs. Macpherson's Class? We went together. You know, that's what we called it. Going together. We were 'going together', and then you dumped me. So maybe it's Gone Together. Or We Went. I'm not sure. I'll have to check on that." He pulled out his little notebook and wrote, I assumed, a note to himself to check on the past tense of the phrase "Go Together".

And all I could think was Holy. Shit. Like, shit in the shape of Jesus posted on eBay. Holy amen Shit.

First Chad Phillips, my lip-locker. Now this. What was wrong with my karma, exactly, and when would the universe finally stop laughing at me?

53

A Brief Digression
While I Reminisce
About 'Going With' Evan Young

6th Grade. Mrs. Macpherson's class. Recess.

I was scaling the monkey bars when I noticed gross Evan Young standing at the bottom of the bars, looking up with wonder. (Then I thought it was just my attention he wanted; now I realize I'd been wearing a corduroy skirt at the time and he was probably checking out the inside of my skirt and the seams of the cable knit white tights.) Evan Young was a dork. His favorite movie was Ghostbusters because it was the only movie that showed what he wanted to do when he grew up: carry around a trash compactor and catch ghosties. He had mounds of dark wavy hair, thick glasses, and a stutter. I always said hi to him because he lived next door to us and my mom threatened me with serious punishments (no cable TV for a week!) if I wasn't nice to him. Unfortunately, Evan thought it was because I was hot for him.

I did a complicated loopey-do-loop spin on the top of

the monkey bars, released, spun three times and landed a solid land. Just like Mary Lou Retton. (In reality, I got tight burn on my legs and fell to the ground.) Evan offered me his hand. "Hey, Chloe. I w-w-w-w- . . ."

I stood up. Wiped my hands off on my skirt and fluffed my feathered hair. "You were what . . ."

"I w-w-w-was w-w-w-w-wondering if you w-w-w-w"

"If I would what?" The popular girls were watching me. They'd never watched me before and I desperately wanted to be cool enough to reenact Madonna videos with them during lunch.

"Go w-w-w-with me."

And there it was. A 6th graders version of full commitment: Going With somebody. It meant seriousness. It meant you belonged to each other . . . sort of like marriage but without exchanging rings or body fluids.

"Sure." I said. "Okay." And then the bell rang.

I think I left Evan glowing on the playground, but I can't remember now. I didn't even like him, I just had never Gone With anybody and I wanted to.

We walked home together.

I imagine we were happy.

We held hands. He told me he really liked my M-M-M-Michael Jackson t-shirt.

We stopped at the door to my house (a lower level apartment with no bath, just a tiny shower.) "Okay," I said. "See ya Evan."

"See yayayaya Chloe."

"No, Evan, I mean see ya. I don't think I can do this any more. I'm breaking up with you."

He didn't say anything. He just slowly took his glasses off, used his plaid shirt to clean them, and then nodded his head.

I never talked to him again and he moved the next summer.

And here he was, mounds of dark hair, big glasses, and cute as could be. But he still wasn't Matt. No one was Matt.

54

Currently At The B.O.B.
With Evan.
Holy Shit, Evan!

"I'm sorry," I said.

"Yeah I was really torn up about it."

"Really?"

"No." There was a pause and then all of a sudden my whole body relaxed. He was joking. At least I thought it was a joke. "We were just kids. It took me a while to place you but I finally figured it out that day you came into Bud & Julie's on that guy's back? You fell or something and he carried you in and you kept sliding off his back."

Oh. God. The day Matt almost-rescued me. I'd been wearing the cutest platform shoes that made me look tall and goddess like (I imagined) and when I got out of his car, I slipped on a rock and twisted my ankle. Pure agony. And then Matt tried to scoop me up but I was afraid I'd give him a hernia, and in an effort to protect our future children, I climbed on his back instead, and instantly started sliding down his back. He managed to carry me into the restaurant with me wrapped around his back like a cat terrified of falling out of a tree. Not one of my smoother moments.

"That's when it all fell into place," Evan continued. Oh yeah. Evan. I'd forgotten about him. "Even back in elementary school you were always doing crazy stuff like that."

I felt a little bit offended. "What's crazy about that? I couldn't help it if Matt was wearing a running jacket. He was slippery."

"No, I mean, you weren't crazy. You were, you know, cute, back in elementary school and you still are. Cute. Quirky. Remember the time you put the broken erasers up your nose to see if they'd fit and they had to call the ambulance? Or during our school picture where you went to the bathroom and tucked your skirt into your underpants? I think I still have that picture somewhere. Anyway. You haven't changed is what I'm saying."

"Oh." I tried to see if I could catch my reflection somewhere to make sure I hadn't forgotten to wear pants or something, but I couldn't find anything. Then I got a little bit offended. What was cute about being rushed to the hospital? Or sliding off a guys back? Or wearing an enormous hat to an otherwise normal party? These were not nice things. These were terrible, wounding, awful things to have happen to a person . . . namely, me.

I didn't know what else to say. I could comment that he wasn't stuttering and that was good, but I was afraid it might come out wrong. Like I was mocking him or something. It seemed like I was all wound up and looking for a fight when I was supposed to be having a good time. But hadn't he just called me cute? That should account for something. We listened to the jazz. I tried to study the menu but ended up just looking around the place.

The jazz was good, and it wasn't too smoky in there, in fact, it wasn't smoky at all. It seemed smoky though. I think maybe my eyes were clouding over with boredom. Evan was all right. I just couldn't focus on what he was saying. He was telling me his life story, beginning with the seventh grade, and I caught snippets of some carpet cleaning business he ran and then going to college for computers and then something about bear sledding? WTF? Bear sledding? Oh, *bob* sledding. Sledding with Bob. Sledding on Bob. Bob bob bob bob. What was wrong with me? Why couldn't I focus on this perfectly nice, perfectly handsome Evan and listen to what he was telling me? Was there something wrong with my ears?

Matt had cute ears. They kind of stuck out a little and the bottom of them were like little tiny punching bags and I just wanted to nibble on them and then drag my tongue delicately down his neck and that little divot (is that a word?) at the base of the neck. God, I loved that divot, and the strong lines of his chin, how it would be rough within hours of shaving. I'd kiss that divot and then kiss his clavicles. There was nothing sexier than a good pair of clavicles and Matt had . . . What was I thinking? HELLO! MATT WAS MARRIED! And I was a loser.

I tried to focus. I really did.

"If you're thinking of ordering the ssssoup, you might want to reconsider," Evan said. I tried not to notice the sibilance of that question.

I wasn't thinking of ordering soup. First, it was June, and I probably wouldn't think about soup until they started playing Christmas Carols on the radio. And second,

God help him if he knew what I was really thinking. Soup was far, far from my mind, say in Nova Scotia. After all, we were in a jazz bar and everything was all sultry and non-smoky but still moody. What I wanted to order was a mojito so I could feel myself slipping away. Really slipping away, and not just in my head. I wanted my body to slip away. But soup? Ugh.

I decided to play anyway. "Why shouldn't I order the soup?" I said.

"They don't have any."

"Really? No soup?" In a jazz bar. Go figure. I bet they don't have popsicles or lollipops either. Probably just stupid stuff like, I don't know, beer, or wine or A-L-C-O-H-O-L.

He scratched the end of his nose. "Oh, sure, I mean, there's ssssoup, I just mean there's no *cold* ssssoup. In the warm months, particularly July and August, I like to have cold ssssoup, but people just don't seem to serve cold ssssoup anymore. There are lots of different kinds of cold ssssoups. More than gazpacho."

He paused here and I remembered I was supposed to be interested in him and having a conversation with him and not thinking of my breaking heart and a man I could never have. Never would have. In a monotone, I said. "Oh. Really. More than gazpacho."

"Sure! Why I've read about all sorts of chilled sssoups in Gourmet magazine. Curried zucchini ssssoup with a dollop of sour cream." Sssssssoup. Why did he keep saying it like that? He was driving me mad! "Pea ssssoup with mint. And my favorite . . ." If he said it one more time I was going to smack him. "Carrot ssssoup with ginger and honey." I smacked him.

Okay. I didn't. But I wanted to. I really did. He just wouldn't stop. "All the sssoups are chilled. All very refreshing, I'm sure, but I just haven't had it anywhere. Only seen it in Gourmet magazine."

"You could get their soup here and just, like, let it get cold."

He looked at me and didn't speak for a moment. "Say, I never thought of that. I'll be right back. I'll try that. It's potato . . ." DON'T SAY IT, EVAN "sssssoup which I think would be much better in October, but maybe if I let it cool . . ."

"Then it will be *chilled* potato soup," I finished for him. "Ever heard of vichyssoise?"

"I have heard of it!" he said happily. "Actually, I've only read about it. In . . ."

"Gourmet Magazine," I finished for him. Yeah. Great. He nodded, told me he'd be right back and while he went searching for his soup, I checked my watch. I shouldn't have been too concerned about getting hot and bothered over this fellow. He was too chilled himself. And I was still thinking about Matt and his lobes. MMMMMmmmm. Lobes.

55

Maybe Double Jointed Fingers Are Okay,
If Used Properly.

Evan pushed the cold potato soup aside. "I guess it tastes okay," he said, "But I don't think vichyssoise is chunky with bacon and cheese. I think vichyssoise is supposed to be smooth. Velvety. This is sort of gloppy. Cold and chunky. Frankly, this soup is sort of creepy."

I snorted. It *was* creepy and I wasn't exactly sure why. I noticed that after he'd gotten the soup he sort of relaxed himself. Maybe his 's' fetish was really just a case of nerves. Funny. Someone being nervous around me. That was sort of, well, nice. "You know what else is creepy?" I asked sweetly. I guess I was starting to relax too.

"Hmmm?" He cocked his head and smiled at me.

"People with double jointed fingers. I don't understand how they can bend them and twist them like that."

"Like what? Like this?" Evan held out his hands and then his fingers contorted.

"Eeeeek!! That's what I mean! Creepy!"

"Ha!" he laughed and leaned back. He was cute. Odd, but cute. And I liked his laugh. "I never thought of myself as creepy. I sort of think my triple-jointed fingers makes me a secret super hero, without, uhm, the super powers or the hero part."

"Just a secret then?"

"I guess. Still, pretty cool, huh?" he did the finger thing again and even though I didn't want to, I laughed. For a moment an image flashed in my mind of what a man could do with triple-jointed fingers. Hmmm. Yummy. To calm myself, I took a bite of his soup.

"You're right," I said. "It is creepy." I was still thinking about his fingers. Fingers like that could surely explore the inner depths of something . . . i.e. . . . me. Ugh. Stop. Stop it. Say something say something. Do not think about fingers. "The fingers," I said. "I mean not the fingers. The fingers are fine. The soup is creepy, I mean. It's a little uhm, thick. You should come back to the restaurant. I'll tell Julie you want some chilled soup. She's awesome." Whew. That was a close one.

"Okay. How about tomorrow?" He was suddenly serious.

I wasn't serious. I didn't really mean he should stop by Bud & Julie's and possibly see me. I mean, I was extending an invitation as a way of conversation, not as a real invitation. A woman would've known the difference. That's why going out with men was exhausting: they didn't know the secret unwritten coded language that women did. When you say to someone "You should come over sometime" you don't actually mean it as an invitation. You don't really want them to visit you. You just say it to say it. It's like marshmallow conversation: light, fluffy, and totally pointless without the graham cracker and chocolate. But he looked very serious. "Are you serious?" I asked. "You're going to stop by tomorrow?"

But he'd already pulled out his little notebook and started writing: "Cold soup with Chloe. 2pm."

I was doing a mental checklist about tomorrow and I wasn't sure I wanted to see him again at all so I blurted "Not tomorrow. Saturday. Tomorrow . . . I have . . ." What could be so important I couldn't reschedule? "To see my gynecologist."

Pause.

"I'm having an issue."

Crickets.

"Nothing serious or anything. Just an issue. With my gynecologist. About billing."

Blink blink blink.

"But Saturday at two is okay?" he asked. He was either smirking or was using his tongue to dig something out of his teeth.

I nodded and was just about to tell him that I didn't have to see my gynecologist after all. I had an Important Meeting With The Music Center . . . but before I could say anything, he stood up, put a wad of money on the table and then kissed my cheek.

It took me a while to realize he'd actually left. It took me awhile because I could still feel his soft lips against my cheek, and his lips weren't at all like Matt's. Oh no, not at all.

55.5

A Brief Digression
While I Explore Heartbreak
South Of The Border

On my way home, I realized that I was famished so I did the only logical thing: Made a bee line (or is it B-line, what the hell kind of phrase is that?) . . . I went directly to Monster Burrito where they proudly served burritos The Size of Your Head. Really. You'd walk in, they'd eye your brain and make a burrito to suit just you. My burritos generally turned out to be enormous which was both a blessing and a curse.

At any rate, just as I pulled into the parking lot, I saw him. In the flesh. Love of my loins, or whatever that Lolita quote is. Matt. Standing at his car holding a plastic bag stuffed (no doubt) with an equally enormous burrito the size of his head.

My heart stopped. Seriously. I died for about thirty seconds. And then I saw there was a woman with him, taller than me, thin. Amber had changed a bit over the last four months. Gotten thinner, older . . . wait a minute! The woman laughed, tossed her blonde hair and then walked over to Matt where, plastic bag pressed between them, she leaned in and kissed him. She was not Amber. And . . . what . . . what did this mean? What was going on? Why did I have to see him. Again. Kissing someone who wasn't Amber, and also, wasn't me?

I drove home in a blur. Burritos forgotten.

56

The Moment of Decision
Or
What Happens When You Eat Ice Cream While Angry

"Don't sleep with him," Megan said.

She said this even before I'd totally entered the apartment. In fact, it was more like she spoke the message telepathically. "Don't sleep with who?" I said as I closed the door and dropped my stuff and headed straight to the fridge. After not eating soup and sitting and listening first to Evan and then to my own mind with a jazz soundtrack, and then seeing the love of my life with yet another woman, all I wanted was the comfort and oblivion of food. Even heartbroken, I was still famished.

Megan was already there: waiting, arms crossed over her chest, the Den Mother incarnate. "Do not sleep with that guy from the restaurant."

"Evan?"

"His name is Evan?"

I nodded.

"Evan. Yes. It's him I'm talking about. You said you

weren't going to sleep with anyone for a year. And I think it's a good plan. You need a break. You go too crazy over men. You ought to take a break from them entirely."

"Oh, what, like you?" I didn't mean to be snarky but Megan was really close to an exposed nerve right then. I sort of shoved her aside a little bit and opened the refrigerator. She closed it on me. It felt a little good to be pissed at her; then I didn't have to be pissed at Matt.

"I am serious, Chloe. Do not sleep with him. You need a break from Matt and you need a break from men in general. You need to focus on you and your friends and your career and stop obsessing. And yes, for fuck's sake, just like me. I like being single and on my own. There's going to be a time when we're married and pushing out kids, and right now, it's our time. Being single, being alone, on my own . . . it's the best thing that's ever happened to me."

"But you aren't exactly alone anymore, are you?" I could hit a nerve too if I wanted, and right then, I wanted to. I also wanted some ice cream.

"I'm dating, yes. But it's been a long time. It's been a long time since I've felt . . ." She paused and when she continued her voice was very soft and weighted with sadness: "It's been a long time since I've felt anything. And I'm taking it really slow with Chad. More slowly than he wants but I just can't . . . not after . . ." The words just hung there, floating around in the kitchen, and then settled on my shoulders, the profound weight of them stooping my shoulders and making me feel like a real arse. Megan has had her string of heartbreaks too involving 5 years of dating and a broken engagement. It had taken her a long time to nurse those wounds and I, fuckface, had been so focused on myself I never stopped to think about her. And come to think of it, since Eric, she hadn't mentioned any love-lusts in a long time. Not until she met Chad. How could I have overlooked that?

"Seriously," she continued, and then took my hand and looked me in the eye. Normally, this would make me uncomfortable because I'm not a touchy-feely person unless I've paid for a massage, but when Megan did something like this, it was just . . . well . . . Megan. It was comforting. "I worry about you."

I shrugged. "You don't have to worry about me. I'm not going to sleep with *Evan*. I had a nice time and all, he even made me laugh but nothing in me is quivering except my stomach muscles. Either I need to eat or have a big poop. I'm going to try and eat a bowl of ice cream first and see if I feel better." I looked at her to judge her reaction. "I probably shouldn't have told you I needed to poop, should I? Roommates shouldn't tell each other stuff like that."

"Roommates don't," she agreed. "Friends do. Okay. Eat your ice cream first. And remember . . . you only have eleven more months to go. Then you can have sex with Evan. Is that a deal?" I thought she was going to make me shake on it, but instead she pulled out a legal document with three places to sign. This is what happens when you work for an attorney. She folded the paper up, put it in her pocket and left me to my own evil plans.

Eleven months. Eleven months on my own. I could totally do that. Matt be damned. Evan be damned. Men . . . be damned. I grabbed the ice cream.

The sad truth was, I didn't want to damn men, not really. Not wholly. I didn't understand what Matt was doing or who he was doing it with, but I did know one thing: whatever we had wasn't resolved yet, wasn't over. And I knew, the way you know about fate, that I couldn't promise not to have sex for another eleven months. It wasn't going to take eleven months . . . because the fundraiser was only two months away, and it was through the fundraiser that Matt was going to realize it was me he was in love with, not Amber, not the burrito lady, but me, simple, messed up Chloe Knaggs. Queen of Blunders.

Matt had his diversion and I decided that I could have mine too. Evan would do just fine. It was sort of like this: Evan was vanilla ice cream; Matt was a blizzard of ice cream and nuts and chocolate and Butterfinger bars. A blizzard.

It was a fitting metaphor because I've always been drawn to chaos.

57

Apparently, Pimento-Sucking Is A Turn On

Matt says: "Chloe." Just my name in his mouth is enough to set me all aglow. He almost growls it . . . which is, I admit, a little weird because it's awfully hard to growl CHLOE. You sort of sound possessed. At any rate, he says: "Chloe! God, it's so good to miss you. I mean see you. I mean it's so good to see you and I miss you."

This was how my dream started. And even though I was sleeping and I knew I was dreaming, I couldn't help but be all excited. It was just like Matt to have a picnic with me in a romantic city park. Or at least it was just like the Matt of my Dreams.

Focus focus focus.

Matt leans over and plucks an olive from the platter in front of us. My vision zooms in on the olive as he brings it to his wet plump lips, parts his mouth and then gently holds the olive between his teeth and suuuuuuuucks until I hear a little pop! And I know, I just know, that he's sucked that pimento clean out of there. He shows me the pimentoless olive and then pops the whole thing in his mouth.

I can't breathe. He grabs another olive, contemplates it. "You know," he continues, "Marriage isn't at all what I thought it would be. I mean Amber is great. She's got a cheerleader body and is incredibly flexible but she just isn't . . ." he looks at me. I look at him. "She just isn't you, Chloe." Then he pops another olive in his mouth, rolls it around, really tastes it, you know?

And that's it!

That does it! Fuck you, Matt M. or Mmmmm or whoever you are! You are not coming into my dreamland and sucking pimentos in front of me and telling me how much you miss me and how good it is too see me and . . . wait a minute . . . how did I get naked? How did he get naked? How did he and I and him and me get . . . ooooohhhhhhh . . . that feels good. That feels really really good. I'm straddling him, and leaning back so I look all perky and the sun is shining and I can hear cicadas and I can almost feel his big, throbbing "Right there!" I cry, "RIGHT THERE FOR THE LOVE OF GOD RIGHT . . ."

"Darling, please tell me you're having a very good dream otherwise I'm going to have to call a paramedic." Mom was leaning over me, her hand against my forehead, checking my temperature.

This was a really unfortunate way to wake up. I did the only thing I could think of: I screamed.

58

Talk About A Mood Killer

I have since come to the conclusion that all good mothers have an amazing sense on when to intrude on your life at the most embarrassing moment possible. Say, when you're twelve and in the bathtub, legs spread, realizing for the first time that running water feels really good if you can get it to hit in *just* the right spot . . . or when you're playing Strip Scrabble with your boyfriend in high school and he just spelled a really good word so you, of course, have to take off your bra . . . or when you're past thirty having an erotic fantasy about the love of your life where you're a bronco rider and he is, well, the horse. You know, times like that.

"Was it a good one?" Mom asked. "Because I keep having this recurring dream about Matt Damon, only now he's ordering ribs and I . . .".

"Get out, Mom! Get out getoutgetoutgetout!!!"

Subtlety does not work with my mom.

"Mom! Please."

"All right, all right, I just wanted to tell you that I saw

Matt the other day and he asked about you."

She sauntered out of my room and gently shut the door.

What? WHAT!!!

How could she do that? How could she come into my room, interrupt my dream, drop a bomb like THAT and then leave?

Ugh.

There was only one thing to do. Chase the woman down.

In five point two seconds, I was in the living room dressed in the only thing I could find: A shaggy bathrobe and a baggy pair of jeans.

"Chloe? Are you gaining weight? You look enormous in that." Mom said. She was sitting on the couch with Megan on the floor leaning against her knees.

"Mom! Come on! What happened?" I couldn't breathe. Really. My heart was beating so hard that I'm sure it shut off my lungs.

Mom focused and rubbed her hands together. (This is how she prepares before she performs her Reiki: she rubs her hands together to create a friction-generated heat and then heals whomever she touches — so she says).

Rubrubrubrubrubrub

"MOM!!!"

"Oh, all right. We'll do this later, Megan, when I can focus my energy more pointedly." She patted Megan's shoulder to get her to move and she stood up and sat next to my mom on the couch.

"What happened?" I said again.

"Your mom saw Matt and he said he misses you and would like to talk to you." Megan blurted.

That was all I needed. I fainted.

Okay. I didn't faint. But if I were Victorian and lived just on like chicken liver or whatever they ate then, I probably would have fainted.

Instead I just sat down. On the floor. And burped.

Lovely. (Seriously, I must have a problem with gas. No one else I know farts and burps as much as I do. Maybe I just have too much testosterone or something.)

"Tell me everything," I said. "And hurry. I've got to be at the Music Center to make my fundraising pitch in twenty minutes."

59

Things I Wanted Out Of Life
Immediately
Please

I wanted to do the following:

1) Stop thinking about Matt.

2) Stop thinking about Matt telling my mom he missed me.

3) Stop thinking about Matt and my mom's point that he was not, definitely not, wearing a wedding ring.

4) Focus on my pitch to the Grand Rapids Music Center.

5) Create a fundraiser so spectacular that all the kids in Grand Rapids can have free violin lessons and expand their brains and get really smart, while I secure a fulltime job with benefits even in a sagging economy.

6) Stop thinking about Matt and the way he kissed

me.

7) Stop thinking about Matt and the way he kissed that lady at Monster Burrito.

8) A burrito sounds really good right now. Focus.

9) Think about dating someone new. Maybe even Evan.

10) Stop thinking about the way Evan said: sssssssoup.

11) Fuck it. Just stop thinking.

12) Drive to the Music Center without getting in a crash.

13) Tell my mom I love her.

14) Tell my mom she is to never, ever mention Mmm's name again.

15) Stop calling him Mmmm. He isn't Mmmmm anymore. He's just a man. With lips.

60

Why I Shouldn't Choose My Own Mantra

Mom said that making a list might clear my mind, and I found she was right. My mind was clear and fresh as a tampon commercial with women playing sports and high-fiving each other and then going out in white dresses to par-tay. Fresh. Open.

Who was I kidding?

I was nervous as all get out. I had to pitch an idea to Lisa, an idea just twenty-four short hours ago, I'd loved, and now I hated more than anything on the planet save a certain married M Man. I couldn't focus. I couldn't breathe. What was that? What was wrong with me? Why had I suddenly developed a facial tic? I touched my face. Was I having a stroke? I was having a stroke! That's what this was! A stroke!

Ah.

No. Just an eye flutter.

I kept walking.

I just needed to focus for twenty more minutes. Just focus. Don't think.

. . . .
. . . . Not thinking . . . .

So what if my mom saw Matt? So what if his hair was messy and he hadn't shaved in days? So what if he wasn't wearing a wedding ring? So what if he really needed to talk to me? I'd seen him at Monster Burrito and he looked fine. Of course, that was a couple of days ago, and maybe he'd seen me too and maybe that moment had flared something in him. Not like a hemorrhoid, but like, you know, desire. For me. It didn't matter. I had better things to do. He knew where I lived, we were friends on Facebook, he knew exactly where to find me and my heaving breasts if he really wanted to. If. He. Wanted. To. Fucker!! Walk walk walk. Don't think.

"Hi, Chloe!" It was Colleen, the Music Center's terminally perky and authentically friendly secretary. "You feeling okay? You look sort of flushed? Like you're having an episode or something? Are you? Are you having an episode?"

I nodded. "I'm here. To. Talk. To . . ."

"Lisa. Right? Right? Go on down. She's waiting. She's excited. I'm excited! Go on down."

Go on down. Down the long spiral staircase into the basement. Down to my future. No problem at all. Just remember to breathe, right? Just be like a tampon commercial. Be a tampon.

Yes.

Ohhhhhhhmmmmmmmmmmmm . . . .

61

Oh Man, Here I Go . . .

Lisa walked into her office and shut the door. She smiled warmly at me and then plopped down at her desk. "You all right, Chloe? You look like you had too much coffee. You're all jittery."

Jittery! That was it! I wasn't having a stroke at all; it was just too much caffeine. I loaded up on the joe this morning as I was preparing my presentation. Actually, I hadn't really prepared anything. I just freaked out listening to my mom tell me about Matt and how 'distraught' he looked and how something 'seriously karmic' was going on with him. But now, I needed to focus. To zoom in. And I was tired of being a screw up. I actually wanted to do a good job with this. After all, this whole fundraising scheme touched on every important area in my life, and it needed to accomplish three things:

1) Raise a whole lot of money for the club so they wouldn't shut the doors

2) Sound fun enough and plausible enough that I

could keep my freelance gig going, possibly replacing my freelance gig with a I'm A Real Girl! Full-time position

3) Prove to everyone that I could accomplish great things, including getting Matt to regret his choice in Amber and possibly leave her (without hurting her feelings. She really was a nice person.)

I didn't want to admit this, but I felt both humanitarian and heartless at the same time.

"So, what do you have?" Lisa asked. She sat at her desk and leaned forward.

"Well, I wanted something a little unique."

"Yes."

"A little hip."

"Yes."

"A little less Blue Hair and a little more . . ."

"Generation X. Yes. They're the ones with money right now. Okay. Sounds good. So I'm hoping this isn't another silent auction."

"And it's not a tea, or bingo, or a cultural performance."

"You've got me so far. What is it?"

"Do you remember the Happy Place?" Just saying the words made my heart go pitter patter.

"The ropes course where we did team building?"

"Yes. Exactly. I want to have the fundraiser there."

"You want a fundraiser for kids music lessons at a ropes course?" I couldn't tell if she were incredulous or interested, so I just nodded. "In the woods?" she asked. I nodded again. "Holy ship," she breathed and sat back in her chair. She really did say 'ship; she didn't like to swear within the hallowed walls of a musical institution. "I love it.

I do. I love it. Oh, Chloe, this is just what the G.R. Music Center needs! A burst of real energy! Something that will make Beethoven quiver in his grave. Well, maybe not Beethoven" she leaned in conspiratorially, "at least it will make the Board Members quiver. They might hate the idea. But, oh, fudge it, what else can we do? I've tried everything and if we don't bring in some real cash soon, those fuddy-duddies are going to have to join the Grand Rapids Opera Society or the Symphony. They'll have to pay their dues all over again, and their names are already all over this building and letterhead. No. A fundraiser in the woods, traveling minstrels, and a tightrope course? Was that it? I think it's fudging brilliant."

I couldn't breathe. I think I may have been crying. You see? Brilliant!

"If you pull this off," she continued, "I'll offer you a full time job in development. With benefits."

My heart stopped. It was just as I'd dreamed. Benefits. A full time gig. Insurance. A real grown-up independent life. Maybe even a car payment of my very own. Double fudge. "And if it fails?"

"Well then we close the doors, you lose a job, I lose my job and everyone blames you."

"Okay then." I said. "Fudge it."

"Fudge it," Lisa said and winked. She started pulling things out from drawers and piling them up on the desk. Then she dipped beneath her desk, disappearing for a moment, and reemerged holding onto a gigantic brown file folder. "Here's your budget, our contacts, sample timelines and checklists. Of course, we have to check the calendar." She pulled up the calendar on the computer and with her back to me said: "The Happy Place, huh? Isn't that where that Mike guy works?"

"Matt," I breathed. "Yeah. He worked there. Works. I don't know."

"Funny, I always thought he had a thing for you. I'm surprised he never asked you out." She spun around to face me. "How does next month sound to you? It's fast but we don't have a choice. And can you come up with a caterer who can prepare delicious food at cost? Or at no cost?"

My head was spinning. I was still stuck on the Matt comment. "Yes," I said. "I think I can."

62

Another Episode I'm Not Proud Of

I walked out of Lisa's office with a plastic grin shellacked on my face, and with each step my heart boom-ba-boomed a little harder. I thought: What have I done? WHAT HAVE I DONE? Or, like Megan suggested, What the Fuck Was I Thinking?

When I got to The Beast, I grabbed my cell, and tired to text a message to Megan. Basically, all I wanted to text was "OMG. What have I done?" but I couldn't figure out the keys. There was some kind of automatic spelling going on and my short message became "Oogle My Good. When hamburger in dirt." And it took fifteen minutes to get that far! Let's face it. I was past the texting demographic. So I said fudge that too and I just dialed her. "Help!" I said, when she answered.

"You did it, didn't you? You promised the sky and the moon and now you're wondering how to deliver."

"It's worse than that. I promised catered food, music, and Matt M's adventure workplace *for free*."

There was silence on the other end of the line.

"Eloquently put," I said.

Megan said: "Get home as fast as you can."

***

An hour and a half later, I was running my fingers through my hair and biting my nails and Megan was pacing back and forth in my kitchen. Mom was already at the grocery store loading up on cocktails to "Soothe the wounded spirit and calm everyone the fuck down". But I was beyond calming down. I was dangerously close to the Precipice of FUBARness.

"Let me get this straight," Megan said. "Your plan is to call Matt, get him to do throw this whole party for free, and what? Get him to fall in love with you? He's married, Chloe."

Well, sure, I thought, when you say it out loud it sounds pretty self-centered and dastardly. But when it's in your head, when you're like plotting everything out it doesn't feel dastardly. It feels . . . like it's the way it's supposed to be. Like Fate. Like maybe years from now I'll be with Matt and it's Thanksgiving and we're sitting at the table with our kids and they want us to tell them how we met and we say we were friends forever, and then Daddy married someone else (can you believe it?) but then he came to his senses and it's been bliss ever since.

"I wasn't thinking about him at all. Not in that way. I am over him. Didn't I just have a date with Edward?"

"Evan."

"Right. Didn't I just have a date with Evan?"

"And none of this is about Matt? This is just you trying to help out the community of little violin players and work on your career, right?"

"Yeah. Well, duh. Yes. Of course. Yeah." The more I

lied, the plainer it became. I even think my nose was growing. Why, why is it that at the moment you're thinking and plotting all these stupid, pointless things, your mouth disconnects and goes on the defensive? I should have just fessed up. But Megan wasn't supposed to know what I was thinking in the depth of my soul. The depth of my soul was off boundaries, my business, my personal space. Sort of like the bathing suit area. Off limits unless you're invited in.

Maybe I was just crazy.

Because that's what I was thinking. I was thinking about Matt. Always him. You know, just like that Lolita story except insert me for the crazy Herman character, and replace the prepubescent girl with a hot sexy Man-Man, and, well, change all the other details in the story and that was me. And Matt. Love of my loins, lust of my liver, you know how it goes.

I was crazy. No question about it. Just out of my head, wire me up to electroshock treatments, because even though I knew it was ridiculous, and maybe amoral, and just plain wrong on so many levels, I did the unthinkable: I picked up the phone and called him. Just like that.

63

The Trouble With Un-Coffee And Un-Boyfriends

"Hello, thanks for calling The Happy Place, your place for team building and spirit growing. How an I help you?" It was him. It was his voice: slightly Texan, or Californian, or just plain relaxed or whatever peculiar combination his history had shaped; it was him. It was he. Oh, fuck it. It was my Mmmmm. He sounded warm and happy.

"Matt?" I said. "Is that you?" I knew it was, because I couldn't breathe again and my heart was thundering.

There was a pause, a breath, and then he said my name. Just my name.

It was enough.

"How are you?" I asked.

"Good. Okay. Terrible," he said.

"Oh."

"Yeah. Well. I saw your mom . . . did she tell you about it?"

"She did." Pause pause pause.

"Okay. Good." More pausing while I listened to him breathe. Finally, he said: "So. How are you doing?"

"Good. Great. Terrible." I said. We laughed. "And Amber? How is she?" It was the worst conversation I'd ever had. What had possessed me to call him like this? Did I really think he was going to come through for me and donate the use of his business simply because I'd had a crush on him? Did I really care how he was doing? How Amber was doing? A little bit, actually. And there was the picture of him at Monster Burrito . . . but that probably wasn't him at all. Still, it was nibbling at my brain. A little.

"Amber? She's the same. I guess. I don't . . ." He sounded like he was struggling for words. Matt never struggled for words. He suddenly didn't sound like himself at all. Where was his relaxed charm, his bravado, his male-ness? And then he said, softly, so softly I thought maybe I'd misheard him: "Chloe? I've, uh, missed you."

That's all I really wanted. To know I'd been missed. It was as if I suddenly lost ten pounds without even using an enema. I was, yes, relieved. He missed me. I meant something to him. Who cared where we went next, *if* we went anywhere. The fact was that I had made a little handprint on this man's life and he sounded just a little bit sad that the print was all that remained.

"Could we . . .? Do you think we could . . .?" He didn't finish the sentence.

I almost wanted to tell him we never could anymore. We were over. But I did need him. Or rather, the Music Center needed him.

"Do you want to meet for a coffee?" I asked. "Bring Amber if you want. I promise not to do any damage this time." I couldn't bring myself to say "Bring Your Wife", but I know he got the gist of it.

"Coffee?" He laughed. "Don't you mean un-coffee?

Because you still don't drink coffee do you? Or have you changed that much since I saw you last?"

Had I changed at all since he got married? Well, duh, yeah. Of course. I had completely changed. Hadn't I? I mean at the core, I was still the same person, but wasn't something irrefutably broken in me? When I woke up in the morning and looked in the mirror, was I really still Chloe Knaggs, undrinker of coffee, slightly overweight, slightly depressed? Could all of this have done nothing to me? Was I different? Did I meet him for coffee, or un-coffee? It was a huge question. Monumental, really, and I didn't even pause to think about it.

"Yes," I said, and, "You're right. It's still un-coffee. I'm still an un-coffee kind of girl."

"Thank god," he said.

And who the hell knew what the fuck that meant?

64

How Do You Make My Mother's Dreams Come True?
Ask Her To Play Therapist

"Let me get this straight," said my mom. "You want to play Therapist?"

"Yes."

"You. My daughter. Chloe Knaggs. Product of my womb. You are calling your mother because you actually *want* to play Therapist."

"Yes."

"Christ. You really do. I thought I was having a hallucinogenic flashback. I mean who knows what chemicals I absorbed in the seventies. But you really want to play Therapist with me?"

"Yes. Yes, Mom, god, how many times do I have to say it?"

"A few more should do it. I just can't believe it." She sounded so happy. As if I told her I was getting married and having a baby.

"I want to play Therapist, Mom. Now."

"Am I the Therapist or the reason for the pain?"

"You get to be the Therapist this time. I've already worked through the pain with you."

"Super. Be over in ten minutes."

***

Usually when my mom said she was going to be someplace, you gave her a thirty-six hour window to show up. Once, it took her two months to walk up the block because she was distracted by a bus ad, followed it, bought a ticket to San Marco, met someone on the plane, had an amazing vacation, returned home, had the taxi drop her off at the bottom of the hill, and then walked up to my apartment.

Not so today. I called her, she said ten minutes, and then she materialized in my living room, all fragmented for a second like in Star Trek. But really. VVVzzzzzzzzz. There she was. "Shit!" I cried.

"Did I scare you?" she said. "I told you ten minutes. Why are you so startled?"

It wasn't her showing up that startled me, I mean she didn't actually materialize, she just walked in unannounced. It was her hair that startled me. My mom, my sixty-something-never-will-tell-me-exactly mom was sporting a mowhawk. And it was green.

"You guys experimenting at the home again?"

She set down her enormous quilted bag, and then sunk into the sofa. "I was trying to teach Sharon some hairdressing tips. You know, convince her that her life isn't over and she can learn new things. She's not just a wife and mother anymore. You know, show her career possibilities . . ."

"And?"

"Oh, her life is over. She didn't understand a thing. But

I told her it wasn't a mistake, exactly, it was a surprise. A gift from life, and we would make the best of it."

"Which part did she mess up on? The green or the mowhawk?"

Mom looked at me like I sprouted a horn. "The eyebrows, dear. The hair is just perfect. Just what I was looking for."

And then I took a closer look at her. She was missing an eyebrow. It had been waxed into non-existence. "Hmmmm," I said. "You look puzzled."

"It's disturbing isn't it?" She gave me a quizzical look . . . or maybe that was just because of the missing eyebrow. "At any rate, where's Megan and why did you call me? It must be serious if you kicked your roommate out of the apartment." She looked around the living room as if trying to zoom in on a clue.

"I didn't kick her out. She just went out. To get tortillas. Which we are in desperate need of."

"Ahhhhhhh," Mom nodded, channeling Freud I'm sure. "An invented errand to get her away from the scene. Very . . ." she rubbed her chin, stroking an imaginary beard "interesting."

"Mom. Stop. I didn't kick her out, I just . . . wanted to talk to you a little bit, alone. And as much as I love Megan . . ."

"I know. I know," she said and waved her hand in the air either swatting a mosquito or making explanations disappear in the air. "So then. Tell me about your mother." She looked at me expectantly. This wasn't what I'd been expecting. And then I started talking.

65

*A Brief Digression While I Wax On/Wax Off
About My Mother*

My momma was so poor when I was growin' up, I had to wear margarine wrappers for shoes.

Ha! I'm just kidding.

Whenever someone wants to tell me about their childhood, I imagine — and it doesn't matter who is telling the story — the impending poor family from the south upbringing. Maybe I've read too much Tobias Wolf or something. Or maybe it's the idea that a young life isn't interesting unless it's set in the south and there's a little girl named Scout with a dad named Attitcus.

I didn't have that. I didn't even have a dad and I'm wondering now if that were part of the problem. I mean, textbook analysts would say that I have an unhealthy obsession with men who don't want me because I never had a dad.

Uhm. Long mighty sentence, but you know what I mean.

I wanted mom to tell me once and for all a) If I was

screwed up and b) If so, how, exactly, did I get that way. I had a feeling it had something to do with communes and co-ops and the free spirit of a single mom, and I didn't exactly want to blame her, I just wanted answers.

66

Mom, The Guru
She Actually Could Charge Money For This

"It's all my fault," Mom said. "You should blame me."

"I don't want to blame you, Mom, I just want . . ."

"You want to figure it all out."

"Yes."

"You want someone to tell you if you're making all the right choices."

"Yes."

"If you're fixated on this Matt because there's really something there, something worth fighting for. You want to know if every move you make is the one that ten, fifteen, thirty years from now is the move that changed your life and made you happy."

"Well, yeah." She was good at this game.

"Forget it."

Did I hear right? "What?"

"No one can tell you these things. Not your roommate, not your therapist, and certainly not your mother. Not even yourself. You can't *know*, Chloe. No matter what choice you make, you'll always wonder about the one you didn't make. That is, as they say, life."

"Well, that sucks. That's a terrible answer. Where's all your new age mumbo jumbo? Where's the comforting 'Trust yourself' stuff you tell other people."

"I try to make other people feel good because it's a nice gesture. But, Chloe, you're my daughter. To you, I'll only tell the truth. And the truth is, you can never be certain about anything. You can never tell who is going to fall in love with whom, and who is going to get married, and you'll certainly never know which of your choices are the good ones and which were mistakes."

I sat down on the couch. More like deflated into the couch. Like I'd become a marshmallow roasting in a fire and my insides had suddenly liquefied.

"But, sweetie, I can tell you one thing that will make you feel better."

"What's that?"

"Your life? You don't live it alone. And whatever good choices you make or bad choices, you will always have your friends and your family."

"Can I come in yet?" Megan called from outside the apartment. "I've been out here for ages."

I smiled at Mom and ran to open the door. There was Megan, sprawled out on the floor like she'd just finished a marathon or something. "Where's the grocery bag? Didn't you get tortillas?"

"You really wanted tortillas? I thought that was just a pointless errand to get me out of the house. I think I have some gum if you need something to chew on."

Mom brushed past me and helped Megan to her feet. "Who needs tortillas when you can have a Tequila

Sunrise," she said. She moved her hand in front of her as if she were painting an actual sunrise. "I brought supplies in my purse. It will only take a second."

Megan followed Mom in and I shut the door.

So no matter what stupid things I did in my life, no matter who I married or didn't marry, how many embarrassing situations I got myself into, I would always have my mom and Megan there with me.

It actually was a comforting thought.

67

My First Mistake: 2 Nondates

I really shouldn't have scheduled a two non-dates in a single afternoon. What was I thinking? But since neither of them were actual dates, more just meetings really, it seemed like a perfectly natural idea. First, I'd meet with Matt for some un-coffee (hello déjà vu!) and then I'd meet with Edgar. Ethan. Evan. Fuck! His name was Evan! I'd meet him for not un-coffee but, apparently, unsoup and we'd just talk or whatever and then I'd plan my fundraiser and Change The World.

It was an entirely plausible and brilliant plan. In my head. In reality? Not so much.

68

My Second Mistake: Bringing Megan

Megan was grouchy. No, she was grumpy. Who am I kidding? She was just plain bitchy. Stompstompstomp went her feet in the apartment. Slam went the cupboard in the kitchen and then more stompstomping. "What is your problem?" I yelled to her from the living room where I was taking a mini-siesta from my fundraising planning (aka counting the minutes until I could get ready for my un-coffee with Matt). If I prepared too early, I'd look greedy/needy/desperate. I had to prove to Megan that I didn't think it was a date (duh. He's married) and I didn't have an ulterior motives. She didn't seem like she was interested at all with her stomping and I was sort of glad because I'd spent most of the morning discreetly shaving and buffing my body until I glowed like I been dipped in radioactive lotion. But I digress. It's Megan we're talking about here and was she ever in a mooooooooood.

"Again, I ask you, What. Is. Your. Problem?" I flipped a magazine page, careful not to smudge my just-painted-nails. And then she was on me! On top of me the way that

Edward would be on Bella in those Twilight books. Like she was a vampire and I was her own personal bottle of . . . oh whatever. She pounced.

"DO YOU REALLY WANT TO KNOW WHAT MY PROBLEM IS?" she bellowed. And she was right in my face too.

"Did you just eat chocolate? Because your breath smells really good," I said.

She harrumphed. "It's very hard to be pissy around you sometimes, Chlo." She said and then released me. "I'm in a mood."

"Clearly."

"It's just . . . I want my life to be a certain way. I was doing just fine on my own in my little studio apartment."

"You hated that place," I reminded her. She did. It was the size and scent of a cat box.

She shot me a look. "And then what happens? I bust my leg and I get stuck living here."

"You like living here." I reminded her again. She gave me another withering look. Maybe, just maybe this was one of those moments when you're supposed to be a friend and shut the hell up and just listen.

"I ended up *here* and then I followed you *there*." She pointed upward and I knew she met Mackinac Island "And I met *him*" meaning Chad "And now my life is simply miserable." She collapsed on the couch. I tried to make space for her, but her body was half on mine. I looked at the clock. I could now get ready without looking desperate. I needed to wrap this up. I was, really, actually feeling desperate. I needed to show Matt that a) I was gorgeous and just fine without him and b) well, that about covers it.

Focus focus focus I told myself. "So you're pissy

because you're happy?" It was the only thing I could come up with.

"Yes," Megan said. And then she started to cry. "I hate being happy. This is just terrible. I don't know what to do with myself."

So. Yes. My first mistake of the day was scheduling two nondates in a single afternoon. My second? Asking Megan to come along.

But what could I do? She was my best friend and lonely and pissy. Any other action on my part would've been considered selfish.

69

Freakazoid

"Honestly, I'm fine," Megan said. She was clutching the door way with her talons, you know, like a cat trying desperately to stay out of a bath. "I don't need to go with you. In fact, I probably shouldn't go with you on your date."

"It's not a date. I'm just meeting . . ." Oh, god. I had to say his name aloud. "Mmm . . ." I tried again. "Matt." There. Easy breezy. Not a hint of desperation or longing.

Megan looked at me. Studied me. Then released the doorway. "On second thought," she said and brushed herself off, "I think I need to go. You need me with you. You're going to throw yourself at his feet and I'll be damned if I let you do that."

"Oh, I am not," I tried to say nonchalantly. But have you noticed that whenever you try to be nonchalant you actually end up being the opposite . . . which is . . . I guess . . . chalant. I was totally chalant. The ruse was up. "God," I breathed. "What am I thinking?"

"You're not," Megan said. "That's the problem. It's

good I'm coming with you. I don't know how you've survived this long without me." She hooked her arm into mine, and this time, she was dragging me to the car and not the reverse.

On the way to Bud & Julie's, where we'd planned to meet for our un-coffee, I imagined how the meeting would go. Matt and I would make out and Megan would throw flower petals on us. I was practically throbbing when Megan put the Beast into park and it shuddered its dying breath before it rested. She looked at me again. "Don't you dare," she said.

Sometimes having a friend who knows everything you're thinking can be really annoying.

We opened the Beast's doors. They creaked in protest. And then I looked up. And there he was. Looking right at me. Smiling.

70

Me, As Ever, At His Feet

There he was. As beautiful as ever. We looked at each other and then Megan made a sound like 'gawd'. I decided I'd just glide over to him la-di-da and sashay past him and into the bar. I started to glide, my foot caught a weird stone thingy and instead I went flying. I'd like to say that Matt caught me, but I landed at his feet.

"It's like nothing has changed," he said and laughed. And then he scooped me up. I must say, as a woman, it's a very satisfying thing to be scooped up. It's both romantic and comforting that you're not heavy enough to cause a hernia. Then he just held me in his arms for a moment and he smiled and I smiled and he said "hi" real soft and I said "hi" and then I said "would you like to say hi to my vagina too?" er . . . okay. That last part I just thought. I did say "hi" though and then Megan said "Uh, hello?" as in: *Uh, hello? Excuse me? I'm standing right here and you two are ig-nor-ing me.*

Oh. Right. I'd brought her along with me. Probably a good thing. I didn't want to have sex with a married man on the sidewalk in front of Bud & Julie's. Wellllllll. I did want to do that, but I do have some self-control.

"Sorry," he said, and he set me down. I stood eye level with his arm pits and there was that musky man pheromone smell.

Arrrrrrrgggggghhhh! This was torture. Fuck it. Fuckety fuckety fuck it. Focus. Children. Violins. Fundraiser. And not orgasms. Not orgasms! Not love not Love Orgasms. Just un-coffee. "Er . . . ." I said. I shook my head. Tried to focus. "Or . . . ." God. Was I going to say orgasm? Help me Jesus Buddha Mother Earth. Help!

"Oh for crying out loud. End the drama. Get inside you two. Sit down and let's forget the coffee or un-coffee or what-fucking-ever and just get blitzed."

I smiled.

Megan, my dear friend, was at times, better than a deity.

Matt opened the door for us and we were in.

71

The Bombshell
AKA
Evan

This time it was Bud working at the bar. Bud looked just as a Bud should, and I sometimes wondered if it were his real name, or a name he donned like a jacket. He was in his late sixties with a belly, a balding head, and handlebar mustache. And the coolest guy just shy of retirement in the neighborhood. He took one look at the three of us and picked up the tequila.

I love that man. He didn't even say a word or hear a word; he just looked at us and knew that we were a group that needed to get schnockered. For a brief moment I had a flash of him and my mom out on a date, but the shuddered. My mom would give the poor man a heart attack. Best not to play cupid with her. I eyed the shot, the three of us clinked glasses, and then down the hatch.

After doing a shot, I felt a whole lot better. And a little queasy.

We sat down at a booth. I slid in first, leaving room for

Matt to sit next to me, but Megan plopped down before he had a chance.

And then we all looked at each other.

You know, in romantic movies, they never tell you about how plain awkward most of life is. It helps that there's a music soundtrack for everything. Just imagine how painful a montage would be when the couple-falling-in-love is at the ice skating rink, then falling into each other's arms, and then at the beach, and then naked doing the hokey pokey ALL TO COMPLETE SILENCE. That, my friends, is not sexy.

And neither was this un-coffee non-date. It was reality. And the reality was my life was incredibly awkward. Just one awkward moment after the next.

I cleared my throat.

Matt pretended to look at the menu and Megan actually sniffed her armpit. She really did! I glared at her. "Sorry," she said. "I thought I smelled onions."

After an unbearable amount of time, I finally took the initiative. "Matt?" There. That was good. That was a start. At conversation. Or something. He looked at me expectantly. Megan looked at me expectantly. Bud said: "You've got to follow that up with something, doll."

Okay. Conversation. With the love of my life. Who doesn't didn't won't love me and married someone else. Great. Super easy! I cleared my throat again: "Matt. Mattymattmatt. Yeah. And, uhm, you know. Life. Heehee. Whew. Well. Ah . . . How are you?" Every word was like plucking an apple from my throat. It might not look like much when you're reading it, but honestly, talking to him was more uncomfortable than a pap smear. "How is . . ." Say it. Say it. Just fucking say it and admit it to yourself.

"Your wife?"

He looked like he was going to cry. And then he actually used the little point of his napkin to wipe away a tear. I heard a little harrumph escape from Megan and I gave her knee a quick, deep painful squeeze. "Amber is . . ." He sobbed. Bit his lip. "Gone."

What? What did he just say? Was she dead? Was she murdered? Did they find her somewhere weird? How awful. I actually liked her. We'd probably be friends in a parallel universe. Where men didn't exist. But dead. Wow.

As if in response, he continued, "Amber's gone. She's left me. It's over. We're . . ." he did a little internal sob thing that sort of sounded like a frog who wanted to get it on . . . "We're over."

I didn't say a word. You'd think I would have jumped up and cheered or high-fived Megan or hugged him or pretended to be all supportive and understanding but instead I was just quiet. Stupid quiet. And at that moment, Evan walked into the restaurant, up to our table and said "Hey, Chloe. I'm early. Did you order our sssssoup?"

72

Awkward Conversation #1,267

Early? Early! Well, duh! I had scheduled these two non-dates with two hours in between. I looked at my watch to confirm and then realized that Megan and I had been twenty minutes late just to prove a point, and then did a shot, and then sat in awkward silence not saying anything and . . . still. 45 minutes early was pretty inconsiderate. How dare he! And now what was I supposed to do? How could I have a make-out-getting-back-together session with Matt if Megan was there with me accompanied by The Soup Man? I mean, how could we canoodle with these noodles in the way? You get my drift?

Aw, again, I said, Fuck It.

The introductions went something like this: "Matt, Evan, Evan, Matt, Evan Megan, Matt, Megan, Oh fuck it fuck it sit down."

Matt tried courageously to pull himself together. "So," he said, sniffling. He got it together than looked squarely at Evan. I could almost hear the testosterone snapping. And not just off of Matt. "Who are you to Chloe?" Matt asked. Did he actually ask that? I looked at Megan. She nodded. He did ask that.

Evan looked around but there were no other men in the area except for Bud. "Oh? Me? I'm Chloe's boyfriend. It's pretty intense, but we wisely decided we're not having sex until . . . hold on a second . . ." Evan reached into his man-purse and pulled out his notebook, flipped a few pages, and then said "Eleven months, two weeks, three days. That's when we'll consummate it. It's okay though. I'm not in any hurry. Except for some soup. I could sure use some soup."

72.5

Digression, Yet Again

There are moments when you sort of drift out of your body, float above it and just observe. That's exactly what I did in that moment. And then my spirit tried to make a run for it because, duh, my spirit is really smart. If I could've gotten the hell out of that restaurant, I would have. There were, however, two things keeping me there: 1) I wanted to know why, exactly, Amber had left Matt and what that meant for me, and 2) Megan had returned my knee-squeeze with one of her own and had firmly fixed me to the seat. Come to think of it, there was a third reason I wanted to stay there. I was suddenly craving soup too.

Staring at Evan, I suddenly realized this was my chance. I gave Megan a little kick and then a complete shove to force her out of the booth. "Evan! Perfect," I said suavely, "have a seat." I motioned for him to take my seat while Megan shot laser beams at me and then, smugly, I crawled in next to Matt.

The rest of it is a blur. Most of it anyway, except

somehow, I managed to hold a brainstorming session about the music center while my reproductive cells were doing the cha-cha. For while I spoke, Matt's leg touched mine, and then his hand brushed my knee, and then his hand was on my knee, and if I could've just crossed my leg or tilted his hand, it would've fallen directly into my lap, maybe even hitting the luscious spot that makes women weep. But that would require really good aim, and I was never good at video games. Instead I just did what I do best: talked out of my ass while my mind was a million miles away. But this was progress; this was something physical, yes?

It seems stupid now, the little things we talk ourselves into believing are big signs. If only I could've seen Matt for who he was, really, instead of who I wanted him to be. If only I'd paid maybe a little more attention to Evan. Shoot, if only I'd paid a little more attention to me, you know? It would've saved me a lot of future embarrassment. Hence, my nickname, Blunder Woman. You don't call yourself something like that without good reason, and in a few short weeks I was really going to earn the name. Big time.

73

The Next Step

"Thanks," Megan said. We were in The Beast heading home.

"For what?"

"For making me feel better about my life. I was depressed but your life makes me feel better."

"Why?" I didn't need to hear her answer.

"Because it's so fucked up. I love it."

All I could do was groan.

"Was that the worst non-dates ever or is it just my imagination?" I asked.

"I'm not exactly sure what that was but I do know you have some serious thinking to do."

That's all I seemed to do was think. I was all set to replay awkward conversation bits like Matt telling me he was looking forward to seeing me again, alone, and Evan saying perhaps we could move on to the bread loaf portion of our relationship next time . . ., but instead I changed my mind. I was annoyed with my love life, or lack thereof. And while both Matt and Evan had promised profusely (trying to one-up each other) to help me with whatever I needed (did that include cunnilingus?) I was going to focus on work instead.

However fucked up that little meeting had been, one thing had been decided: The Great Rope Course Fundraiser was on, Matt was donating use of the Happy Place, Megan wasn't grumpy anymore, and Evan had promised something that involved loops and yoga lessons or something (I wasn't really paying attention to him). What did this mean? I had a lot of work to do. The first thing to do, would be to choose a new name, because The Great Rope Course Fundraiser was about as bad a name for a fundraiser as the Great Enema Blow Out.

I'd need reinforcements.

"Call your mom," Megan said. I was already pushing the buttons.

74

Megan's Cure All: A Nudie Bar

"We should drink those blue turtles or something," Mom suggested.

"Flaming Turtles," I corrected.

"Whatever. It's either hard to brainstorm sober or I'm coming down with a case of dementia."

"It's both," I said.

We'd been brainstorming for ten minutes and already my apartment was strewn with crumpled up pieces of paper and little puffs of smoke were seeping out of Megan's head. "This sucks," she said. "Let's do something interesting."

"I can't," I said. "I've got to work. I'm really trying to focus here. I'm trying to be responsible. To stop thinking about Matt or men or Mmm or even the Soup Man. I'm trying to . . . What are you doing?" Megan was looking frantically for something in the drawers.

"I'm looking for a number."

"A number for what?"

"The best way to brainstorm on something is to stop

thinking about it. To focus on something else. So that's what we're going to do. We're going to the Tropics. Where we can all forget for a while."

"And what, exactly, are the Tropics?" I had a vision of Mom, Megan and I hot-tubbing together. It was a little odd.

Mom piped right in. "It's a nudey bar. And if Megan and I are sharing the same thought and I think we are, then I think tonight might just be Full Frontal Male Night."

Megan nodded. "And I need the number. I can't quite remember how to get there."

75

A Note, A Whisk, & Mmm

Pendulous.

That's the only word I can think of to explain that experience. The men were pendulous and . . . uh . . . well groomed. I had never really considered a man's genital area as landscaping, but apparently, with the right hairdresser (one they really trusted I'd guess) it was. On second thought, maybe the word was: bulbous. Pendulous, bulbous, swinging . . . Really. I could probably comfortably give up sex for two years after a night like that.

I turned the volume up on the TV. A rerun of Mad Men. I'd seen it a dozen times which was perfect. I didn't want any plot right now, just to imagine myself in 1950's clothes.

You know, Megan was right. Staring at a few naked Johnson's really got my mind off of work and landed me right into inspiration. We'd call the fundraiser:

Balls to the Walls: Raising Funds for Kids and Getting it Up!

Hmmm.

Maybe I should sleep on it.

I reached into my purse for a stick of gum to get rid of the taste of vodka and cranberry juice, and that's when I found the note. "What the?" I breathed. Tucked in my purse, maybe nestled in there since the morning of the un-dates, was a little tiny piece of paper with the words "I want to whisk you away . . . anywhere."

WTF?

I mean, really, What. The. Fuck? Or more precisely, who the fuck? Who the fuck wanted to whisk me? Me? Someone wanted to whisk me? I had always wanted to be whisked. I called for Megan but she was passed out in her room after a drunken phone call (punctuated by heavy breathing. I didn't ask.) to Chad. And we'd already dropped my mom off at the retirement home to, er, retire.

There was only one thing to do: hold the note in my hand, and fantasize about Matt writing the note. Of course he had written it. I knew Evan had paper and all, but clearly, it had to be from Matt. Because hadn't he locked eyes with me and sent me those signals . . . Hadn't he said, "Let's talk about the fundraiser tomorrow. Alone." And hadn't he said it just a little bit pleadingly?

Aw, fuck it. I didn't care who sent the note.

It was the best thing I'd ever received. And I didn't even have to imagine myself dressed up like a 50's movie star. Someone, maybe even Matt, right now, might me dreaming about me. And a whisk. And . . . mmmm. Enough said.

76

Priorities

What I needed to do was focus. So I went to the refrigerator and ate a scoop of Chunky Monkey and Whiplash Brownie Sundae and floated on a sugar coma for an hour . . . then I opened the first file on the Leaning Tower of Pisa that Lisa . . . Pisa and Lisa rhymes (hehe), had given me. She'd given me the history of all their fundraisers and checklists of things to consider, i.e. : name of event, location, ticket price, tickets, entertainment, food, fundraising opportunities within the event, guest list, target donors . . . it went on and on. It sort of turned my stomach. "Target Donors" made me think we'd be asking for not just their wallet but their kidneys, heart and lungs too.

I spent two hours mired in planning and didn't think once about being whisked (it was closer to ten times, but I was still very focused) and I came up with my own list which I slipped into a pink folder on which (more whiches) I'd glue-gunned sequins in the shape of a violin. I was not my mother's daughter for nothing. And on my list was the following:

1) Name TBA by me.

2) Location and venue: Discuss with Matt. Alone. With whipped cream and whisks of varying sizes.

3) Entertainment: Mom's territory.

4) Food: Talk to Julie & Bud

5) Tickets: Money. Which sounded difficult, boring and legal. Toss to Megan.

6) Guest list: No idea. I guess that's mine.

7) Meet with Lisa once event is in planned and in motion.

8) Do this by tomorrow morning 8am sharp.

Easy breezy. A quick glance at my watch told me I still had ten hours to accomplish everything on my list. I'd just have a little bit of wine, make some phone calls, stop at Meijer for sex supplies for Matt and I, wake up at 7, meet with Lisa at 8 and stun her into silence.

First the wine. Then victory.

77

The Morning After 'Priorities'

"Oh, Jesusmaryandjoseph! The leprechauns are attacking! They're biting my ankles!!!!!!"

That's how I woke up.

And it wasn't a league of leprechauns attacking. It was my alarm clock buzzing. Oh, fuckety-fuck. I reached for the checklist by my bed: "I want to whisk you away anywhere". Ugh. Not that one. The other checklist. I quickly scanned it to see how much I'd accomplished before having a little drinkypoo and collapsing in my bed.

Exactly.

What I thought.

I accomplished exactly nothing.

All right then. I could handle this. No problem. I still had two hours to get myself together, make a couple of phone calls and get over to the music society. Then there was a knock on my door and Megan peeked in.

"You know there was a time change last night, right?"

"Whaaaaaaaatttttttt?" The roar emerged form me the way I imagine the Hulk emerged from Dr. Whatshisname.

"I'm just messing with you." She said, smiling her big shit-eating-Megan smile. "Where's your list? Let me see if I can help you."

GodBuddha bless roommates.

Megan went over my list while I tried to multitask while getting ready. There are certain things you should never multitask and I quickly learned that sitting on the toilet and curling your hair at the same time (while eyeing the People magazine at your feet) really didn't mix. I learned this because within seconds I had a long scorch mark above my eyebrow, making me look like a Vulcan-wannabe or someone who was terminally surprised. "Fuckety!" I screamed.

"Poop. Then curl," Megan hollered back. "How many times do I have to tell you? Poop! *Then* curl!!!"

She was right.

Fuck. Why was I so irresponsible? Why did I have a drink last night? Why did I seem able to commit to only one thing: an unrequited love for a newly dumped Mmm? Pathetic. Seriously. And just when I was starting to get it together . . .

The door opened. "Get it together," Megan said. "I've got half your list done. We can accomplish the rest of it in The Beast."

I nodded. Shimmied out of my pajamas, pulled on something from the bathroom floor and we were out the door.

78

Why You Should Never Wear Your 'Going Out' Clothes Out In Public

I was sitting in the principal's office and he was just about to tell me I was suspended for mooning the choir teacher. Surely, that's what was about to happen. Again. Only this time, I was thirty (coughcough) instead of thirteen and the balding principal had been replaced by the brilliant Lisa.

"This your list?" she asked in a manner that was devoid of any emotion. Like even sophisticated analysts like my mom and Megan and me couldn't read anything into her flat delivery. So I did the only thing I could. I nodded. The clock ticked. I heard a distant piano being tuned. Come to think of it, it was rather creepy sitting in the basement office of the bowels of a music society listening to one piano note banging over and over and over. It was very Hitchcock. (And then I wondered if Hitchcock's friends would call him Hitch or Cock, you know, like endearingly?)

"You still with me Chloe?" Lisa asked in that same flat

tone voice.

"Huh? Yep. I'm here. Just . . . you know . . . my mind . . . Buzz buzz. Details."

She nodded.

I waited. Looked at my shirt and realized I'd pulled on the same shirt I'd worn to the tropics. The shirt my mom and I had made with puffy paint that read "Hump Me I'm Irish". We'd thought it was hysterical because a) the word 'hump' and b) the word Irish. But Moon Goddess, I was wearing it to an office meeting. When would I learn? WHEN?

"It's fudging brilliant," Lisa said, interrupting my thoughts. "Everything's a go. Get on it. Go. What are you waiting for? GO!"

Oh. She really meant for me to go. I stood up, grabbed my sequined file folder and hugged it close to my chest, hoping she hadn't read it. Just as I reached the door, she called out to me "One more thing there, Chloe?"

"Ehm, yes?"

"Could you make me one of those shirts in a medium? I'd like to wear it to the next Mensa Meeting. There are a lot of single guys there, and they don't handle subtleties well."

"Sure thing," I said, and then I gave her the thumbs up.

I actually gave her the thumbs up.

Ugh.

78.5

Digression #23
Conversation With Matt
AKA Fodder For Therapy

It's at this point that I have to take a little digression, not exactly a U-turn or what have you, but a little pause while we go down this misadventure road to tell you about a conversation I had with Matt. I'm doing this, yes, in self-defense because when you analyze what he said to me, how he talked to me, maybe then you can understand why I went out of my head. And when I look back on it, it seems ludicrous that there was no physical intimacy happening. And I mean none. No more lip smacking, hand holding, or naked pubis areas touching. No dry humping either, the kind that I made Ken and Barbie do when I was a girl. We were just friends, with hinted at benefits. With Matt, it was always hinted at. In my defense, I offer this conversation taken word for word (which means pieced together from my splotchy memory) that happened a few days after my meeting with Lisa when everything was still in the planning session.

I went over to his house, which had returned to its former bachelor appearance, where Matt had a dinner all ready for us, sitting on a table with two candles lit. The curry was still in the takeout containers, but I found this profoundly romantic and not a symbol that he wasn't taking me serious.

After curry and chit chat, here's the meat of our conversation that night that we had while I snuggled in his arms between the commercial breaks of The Daily Show and The Colbert Report:

Matt: This feels good.

Me: What?

Matt: You. Here with me.

Me: Mmmm.

Matt: And there's something I've been wanting to talk to you about.

Me: Yeah?

Matt: No, don't look at me. Just look forward. I just want to talk a bit okay? I just want to ask you some hypothetical questions.

Me: Er, okay.

(I have to say at this point I was in deep danger of throwing up our curry dinner because my nerves were going absolutely bonkers.)

Matt: Let's say you were really good friends with someone and you'd never, say, crossed a line with them physically.

Me: Yeah?

Matt: Do you think if you crossed that line that you could still be friends with them?

(WTF? In Matt-speak I figured out he was asking me if we slept together would it change our relationship. No. It would not. Fuck me now!! Ahem. Sorry for the outburst. I very gently and slowly said the following:)

Me: If you are very good friends, true friends, real friends, then maybe crossing the line will actually, uhm, enhance your relationship. Maybe you will find something even more wonderful than friendship.

(Subtext here: Maybe you will find love.)

(Matt turned my face to look at him then, and then kissed my forehead. It was a wildly chaste gesture.)

Matt: You're the coolest girl I know, you know that?

Me: Yes.

Then we continued to snuggle until I fell asleep in his arms. An hour later after he'd shaken me asleep, I was in The Beast on the way home dreaming of the time when we'd finally, at long last cross that line. Surely he meant soon. Right?

79

To Sum Up: Something Jacked Up Happened

I'm not going to go into all the boring details of planning an exciting, never before heard-of event to raise funds for a little musical organization because . . . drum roll . . . it's so intensely boring you start playing Hangman with yourself. And you already know all the words, because, duh, when you play with yourself you're both brilliant.

Hmmm. That didn't quite come out right.

Let's just say that I was working. Actually working. Focusing on little details like what an invitation should look like and how to get a buzz going on Facebook without actually being buzzed. And meeting with Bud and Julie to determine the menu. And talking to Megan about logistics. And Evan and I were also meeting to eat, what else, pureed soups across town. Even my mom chimed in. She offered, free of charge, to tell fortunes at the event and since I'd thrown everything else in, I decided why the hell not . . . except she must promise to wear clothes, not eat mushrooms, and refrain from any Kama Sutra discussions.

I'd met with Lisa at the Music Center to bang out all the details while trying to control my fear at the low ticket sales. Lisa said: "One thing you'll get used to in fundraising, Chloe. You never know if an event is going to be a success until the night of. No one buys tickets ahead of time. There might be ten people there; there might be hundreds." Both options made my stomach roll over and play dead.

And then there was, of course, Matt. We were meeting all the time again and it felt . . . normal. Just like it'd always been. Of course, there was no mention of line-crossing or even line-tiptoeing again, but every time he saw me, he just lit up. Or maybe he was lit. I'm not entirely sure. At any rate, it was exactly the way it had been Before. Before Mackinac Island, Before Amber, Before the stupid Kentucky Derby Incident.

It was, ho hum, exactly as it had always been: a friendship that had a strange intimacy without, ever, any intimacy whatsoever. The only change was that now whenever I saw him (notebook and file in hand, a pretext of event planning), he seemed to be eating like garlic bread or bagels dipped in garlic or deep fried garlic balls, as if I were a vampire. I did want to suck . . . his face . . . but I had some self-control, didn't I?

Yep. It was exactly the same. Just the same. Me and Matt and, unfortunately, no whisking. Not a single beater.

If it weren't for the constant activity I might have noticed that my relationship (or un-relationship) with Matt was rather lame.

What I needed, what I wanted was something crazy, something messed up, something based on bad reasoning. I wanted something fun. And even Matt's sexy voice and pheromone popping clavicles weren't doing it for me. Something had stopped . . . and I was increasingly worried that it was my sex drive. Maybe all this non-ness with Matt was having its effect: I was going strangely numb. And that was strange, really, the sudden realization that Matt, sitting next to me, arm wrapped around me, wasn't, uhm, doing it for me. Or my . . . dare I say it . . . yes I must say it . . . this time I will embrace this word without actually embracing it . . . he wasn't doing anything for my . . . Vagina. He wasn't doing anything for my Vagina. Poor girl. No. There wasn't anything going down there when I was around him.

But one day those juices did get flowing, and yes, I realize that's a gross description, and yes, there is such a thing as too much information, but this is important. Because one day, the night before the big event, the night before the night that would change my life forever . . . something strange did happen.

And her name was Amber.

. . .

. . . . .

. . . .

Hmmmm.

. . . .

. . . .

I realize that might sound like I met Amber, connected again with my clitoris and she and I lived happily ever after. Together. But again, I must repeat, that although the idea of being a lesbian seems a whole lot easier, the actuality of being a lesbian just didn't work for me. And now that I think about it, who's to say that being a lesbian is any easier really? It's still about love and lust and chemicals and emotions and no matter who you are, that's a recipe for disaster. Or therapy. Or both.

I digress. I've got to stop digressing! (Which is another digression.)

But Amber did, in a strange way, get me reconnected with myself . . . and it was that reconnection that caused the sparks that led to the night . . . Aw, fuckety. I'm starting to sound like "This is the house that Jack Built."

So, to sum up: Something jacked up happened. And it started with Amber.

Nothing too mysterious about that, is there?

80

Another Reason I Should Switch To Netflix

Megan and I were at Modern Video which, yes is an anachronism, but there were moments in life when you needed a good 1950's melodrama and you couldn't wait to organize your Netflix queue and wait to have it delivered. That required *planning*. And a night of 1950's melodrama wasn't someone one planned: it was something that was thrust upon someone. Like this night. Modern Video was there for us, with all the cheap VCR rejects that people had abandoned for their DVDs and blue rays.

Megan was depressed because she was falling in love with Chad and she didn't want to be in love; I was depressed because I was still sort of in love with Matt but nothing at all was happening; so the best thing to do was to be together and bawl madly over the closing scene of Madame X, a truly divine movie starring Lana Turner of a good-woman-gone-bad-but-in-a-great-way. We needed this movie. We were looking forward to it, anticipating it the way we anticipated a serving of the Vulcan Volcano at Bud & Julie's.

But it wasn't on the shelf. How was this possible? And then I saw it, actually saw my movie that I was destined to rent in the grimy paw of a tallish woman with frizzy red hair, twenty pounds extra weight, and a big pimple on her chin. And weird, but she was wearing a t-shirt I used to have that said U.P. Yours. I missed that shirt. Whatever happened to that shirt? Hmmm. Come to think of it, the woman sort of looked like me. Exactly like me. Only taller and then Holy Shit (like holy-Mother-Mary-in-a-tortilla) I realized who it was. Amber. In the flesh. A lot of flesh. And looking profoundly happy.

"Megan," I breathed. "Megan," I hushed. "Megan!" I bellowed because, well, that's what I did.

"You don't have to yell. I'm standing right next to you."

And then I pointed. And strange enough, at the same exact moment, Amber lifted her finger and pointed at me. At me! "You!" we said.

Weird.

I swear these kinds of things only happen to me. I mean, who would've thought that out of the blue, I'd see who was at one time my nemesis, picking out the same exact movie I wanted at a dead-end video store? But it's true. I tell you, honest to god, it's true. And the even weird thing is she was with someone who looked a lot like Megan, only in miniature. Literally. In miniature. Her friend was a Little Person wearing tiny little jeans and her brown hair teased up in homage to the 80's, and a scowl that looked distinctly like Megan's.

We all stared at each other in disbelief because, well, what the hell else are you going to do in a situation like that? "So?" I said at long last. I scratched my elbow. I find that in tensely awkward situations if you scratch something, anything, it becomes a lot more bearable. Gives you something to do until you can think of something brilliant to say. "You guys want to go out for a drink with us? We can arm wrestle for that movie."

Megan looked at me. Amber looked at me. Little Megan looked at me. Even the video clerk looked at me.

"Okay," Amber said. "Sweet."

And we were off.

Fuckety.

81

A Brunette, A Redhead, And A Midget Walk Into A Bar . . .

We walked across the street to Logan's Bar because a) it was a cool, woodsy type bar with amazing sandwiches and big drinks and b) it was right across the street. The place was hopping and we found a cozy little corner where the four of us could squeeze in uncomfortably. After about forty seconds of pure silence, the Little Person, whose name was Ivy said: "I hate this. I don't know what the hell is going on between you two, but I'm in therapy right now and this is totally going to set me back. I'm going to go to the bar for a round of drinks and I'll come back when you two . . ." she pointed her little fingers at me and Amber "sort this weird shit out."

Without pausing to breathe, Megan said: "I'm coming with you. I'll buy."

So the two of them abandoned Amber and I (or me, I never know which one it is), anyway, me and Amber alone except for the ghost of Matt sitting distinctly in between us.

Amber rolled up her sleeve and put her elbow on the table. "You ready?"

Was she serious? She seriously wanted to arm wrestle? What could I say? I shrugged. "Okay." We locked hands. Suddenly, the bar quieted to a hush with everyone staring at us. (Okay. This next part may have only been in my imagination but just humor me a bit. A girl needs some action in her life when she has, uhm, no action in her life). So. The bar quieted to a hush and Amber and me (or I) locked hands and locked eyes. "I'm gonna take you down," I said.

"Beeeee-iiiiitch," Amber said.

Okay. Actually, that's not what happened at all. We started to arm wrestle, but because physically we were pretty well matched we just sort of held hands. In the really busy bar. I think I sweated a little.

"So are you still married?" I asked, trying to be oh-so-cool.

"Still? Not still." She said.

"Oh," I said. 'Not still'. What did that means? "Okay," I said and I tried to make it sound like everything was fine and not like my heart was exploding in my body which was exactly what it was doing. Matt was available. Available! But why? And why hadn't he talked to me about it? Why hadn't he kissed me again? Why hadn't he let me touch the sharp line of his jaw with my tongue? Huh? What was up with that.

"He has a small penis," she said, as if this explained everything. And then slammed my hand down against the table. "And I fell in love with a woman. That woman." She turned and pointed to Megan. Correction. She turned and pointed to Little Megan who was looking at us with the slow burn of an intensely jealous person. Hmmm.

82

Opening The Box
(Pandora's Box That Is)

You know, alcohol is all fun and games until someone gets knocked out. By a midget. Really, I should've seen it coming, but that Little Megan was a demonic little fuckety with a mean upper cut, an upper cut, mind you , straight up in the air, knocking my jaw back and causing, I'm sure, an instantaneous bruise . . . sort of like Gorbachev's wine spot, only in the chin area. "Holy mother of . . ." I started, rubbing the hair on my chinny chin chin.

"Salomé!" cried Amber.

"You little shit!" cried Megan. And then *she* leapt. Well, really she didn't leap, she sort of fell downward, pinning the anger-management potential client straight to the sticky floor of Logan's Bar.

Man. That hurt. I mean, it really, really hurt. And what the hell? What was happening to me? Was I crying? Yes! Yes I was. And there was Amber, patting my back, and Megan, and even little Salomé peeled herself off the ground to comfort me. "I just can't take this any more!" I wailed. "Not the pressure of Matt or this stupid fundraiser or my mom or friendship or being attacked for no apparent reason or . . ."

"Sorry about that," Salomé said. "I have a few issues I'm working on."

"Is there anything we can do to help?" asked Amber. "I mean it. You did me a huuuuuge favor up in Mackinac. I've been wanting to thank you for months. Is there anything I can do for you to help you?"

I looked at her, and the tears miraculously dried up. Seriously. And I took a deep breath and said very distinctly, "Actually, Amber, there is something you can do for me."

Then I paused.

Look, this was a dramatic moment and I wasn't about to let it slip away from me unawares.

"Okay," she said. "You name it."

"You can tell me the truth. All of it. I want to know . . . everything."

I'm sure there's a biblical story somewhere about someone wanting to know too much and then turning into a pillar of salt or something. Or, no, wait. Pandora's box. Pandora should never ever have opened her box. Box. She opened her box. (Why! Why must my brain always go into the gutter. Undersexed that's what.)

I really should have gone to Sunday school. Maybe then I would've known better than to ask for the truth, because the truth? It will bite you every time, and that bugger has sharp teeth and is even stronger than a mean little dwarf.

83

The Truth, The Whole Truth And
Nothing But The Truth . . . Sucks

"I didn't know a thing about you. Not at first," Amber said. By this time we had all gotten control of ourselves with a little help from a peachy shot compliments of the bar. "Matt never said a word about you." She put her hands softly on top of mine and looked into my eyes. There was kindness there and it kept me from fainting, or growling, or just plain crying. "He never said anything. We broke up because I needed some space. Maybe I always knew that Matt, that men, weren't right for me, and during that time I . . . explored a little, but I was still unsure. So I went back to Matt because it was . . ." She searched for the word.

"Easy," I offered. She nodded her head. And if you think hearing that her 'easy' was my 'dream' well, what's that phrase? You've got another think coming. It was agonizing to hear her say it.

"But when you showed up on the porch that day, I took one look at you and I knew. I just *knew*." She raised her hand in a motion, like she was painting something in the air only I just couldn't make it out. Either she was a really bad mime or the midget punch and peach shot were taking hold of my brain.

"What did you knew?" I asked.

"Know." Megan corrected.

I nodded slowly.

"I knew there was something between you. You two . . . shit . . . talk about sparks and energy and what have you. He said there was nothing there, but jeez, even I felt it. Even I thought you were . . ." she paused her and looked at Salomé, "even I thought you were cute. And I sort of went ballistic about it."

I was smiling. Suddenly and profoundly smiling. You see? It wasn't all in my imagination, there was something between me and Matt. Something tangible. Something like . . . I tried to paint a ghost heart in the air but I was feeling profoundly hazy. Something still wasn't right here. If there was clearly something between Matt and I, why did they elope, why did he choose her over me? I still couldn't figure it out. And what about last week, his heart-to-heart conversation about crossing the line with me? Huh? I'd been going out of my head analyzing that one and I was certain that the connection between us would be . . . consummate, and soon. I was counting on it. But what if . . .? My mind was struggling to piece things together.

"Amber . . ." I began tentatively, wiping the cobwebs delicately from my mind. "You guys did get married though, right? I mean, you are married now."

Amber shook her head and laughed. "God, no. That's what I wanted to thank you about. I sort of had an epiphany in the gallows. I just didn't want to be perfect anymore. I wanted, I guess, to be more like you. Or more precisely, I wanted to be more like me, and after that night with you in the gallows, I figured it out."

"The lesbian thing?"

She laughed. "For starters. But more than that. I just, I don't know, decided to relax and stop fighting my life so much."

Huh. That was a pretty cool realization, I thought, and then I thought "Wow. They weren't even married. She left him."

But wait a minute here. She left him. So why did it take him six months to get ahold of me? What was the trouble with the timeline here? Unless . . . six months was around the time someone started feeling profoundly lonely, if no one else moved in to take up the extra space in your heart. I was feeling profoundly lonely all the time.

That's when the Truth gave me the second sucker-punch of the evening. The truth was, I wasn't imagining anything, something had existed between me and Matt, and he knew it. He capitalized on it, and he was an asshole for keeping me on a string.

Then I passed out.

Seriously.

It was a one-two KO for little Salomé and a big realization. The man of my dreams . . . was a dick.

84

Fuckety
Or In The Words Of An 80's Power Ballad:
Love Hurts

Okay. So I am being a little dramatic here, but I feel like I've earned that right. I didn't really pass out . . . I just sort of . . . blinked. For a really long time. I just leaned my head back, closed my eyes, and all the pieces clicked together. You know how in "The Sixth Sense" in the end Bruce Willis finally sees that he was a ghost the whole time? And I'm not ruining anything here because that movie is like decades old. But it's this quick movie montage where you see him trying to open the stuck door, and you look closer and it's because the door isn't stuck, there's a bookshelf in front of it. And underneath his jacket there's a bullet hole.

It was as if I suddenly realized I had a bullet hole that went right through my heart. All the evidence was there: Matt's hesitation to let me really into his life; his insistence that we were soul mates or what have you; his collection of girlfriends; his sudden elopement with Amber; his sudden turnaround to me, telling me again that *we* were soul mates. You see? You see what I'm seeing here? Matt was the door and I was the bookshelf!

No. That doesn't make sense.

Here's the truth. Matt did not want me. Not the way I wanted him. I was his friend and only his friend. And he'd kissed me those few times more because I initiated it, because if he didn't kiss me he might risk losing me. The truth was, I was Matt's Back Up Plan, along with a host of other girls, girls I'd seen at his party, girls I even saw on the course up in Mackinac, girls like the one outside Monster Burrito, girls like I'd probably see tomorrow night at the fundraiser. Girls loved Matt and he needed them. And I was the ultimate non-girlfriend. Always there, always looking at him as if he were the best thing since Batman. Adoring him. A constant ego uplift.

"Hey, Chloe. You in there!" Megan was tapping my cheeks, and then she whacked them. Really hard. Man, I was really getting beat up here.

I opened my eyes. For the first time, I opened my eyes. "Oh, yeah," I said. "I'm here."

I didn't mean it to sound like a threat, but it certainly did. And maybe subconsciously it was because the next night, the night that would decide my fate with the music society (an actual career) and the fate of my love life (Matt or no), that night was tomorrow, and I was about to do something very threatening indeed. It began harmlessly enough: "So, you and Salomé doing anything tomorrow night?" I asked.

They looked at each other. They looked at me. "I guess we are now, huh?" Amber said.

"Oh, yeah," I said again. "Definitely. You're doing

something."

After another toast, the four of us walked out of Logan's bar, all thoughts of Madame X forgotten. We walked in slow motion so we looked super cool, like the cast of MI5 or Mission Impossible. We walked across the street and then got in our cars and went back to my apartment to plan. For the big night. Grand Rapids Music Center's fundraiser: Kicking It Under the Stars. Where I would, once and for all, seriously kick it. And by kick it, I mean Matt. To the curb.

85

The Set Up

In movies, no matter what time of year it's supposed to be or the weather or if it's in the Dust Bowl or in a Jungle, streets are always clean and washed, glistening black so that you can see your reflection. It's movie magic, the way they can transform an alleyway into, I don't know, a dream lane or something, where even the hookers sparkle.

The night sort of felt like that. At first. I arrived at The Happy Place at 2pm for set-up. No one was supposed to show up until at least 6pm, but I was, well, a nervous wreck. I had to get control of my emotions . . . and more importantly, I had to get control over the event. I'd spent a good portion of the previous night making phone calls to certain women inviting them to show up at the event. This would serve me in two ways: boost the attendance, and help out in the Matt area (which I'll explain later).

Now I was just trying to hold it all together and not go crazy. So much was riding on this night. And if I didn't have a sense that the night was going to be successful, if there was even the hint that only ten people were going to show up, I had my mom and Megan cracking their knuckles in the background just waiting to wrangle up some people. And Chad had come down to help, of course. And Bud (dressed in his Harley outfit) and Julie from the restaurant, Julie's husband Dan, along with Julie's best friend Eve, her twin boys, and Eve's husband Kevin. They were setting up mountains of sci-fi themed food along with brochures for their new catering business. And Evan showed up too, looking like he just woke up and scribbling notes frantically in his notebook. "Okay, Chloe, what would you like me to do?" He asked, pencil poised. Before I could answer, he said: "You want me to clean up? Get some people? Go shopping? What?" I hesitated to have him hang lights but he said he was good on the high wire and so, well, I wanted to see him try it.

At 3pm, Evan was hanging upside down in the tree branches, creating whirlwind masterpieces with Christmas lights, mom had set up a table for fortune telling, and the food they started bringing in smelled divine: miniature Vulcan Volcanoes, and a gigantic sandwich looking very much like Jupiter, alien creatures created from soft pretzel dough. Things were moving. And by 5:30, we were just about ready to go . . . but I couldn't find Matt anywhere. I wasn't just looking around for him for selfish reasons, he'd volunteered to run the ropes course and he was really good at schmoozing with people so I was hoping he'd convince some donors to, you know, cough it up.

As I looked around, I smiled at the weird collection of people I called my friends and family. Here, in my hour of need, they all were. I even had Amber and little Salomé waiting in the wings along with thirty or so of Matt's closest non-girlfriends. And everyone was working together not just to put on a successful event, but to support me, to help me, to say to the world "Chloe is a fuck up, but she's our fuck up." It was enough to make a girl misty-eyed.

But, Matt?

No. No Matt. Not a clavicle in sight.

If the universe was trying to tell me something, I finally got the message. And not a cryptic message written by who-knows, about whisking me away somewhere, and not strange conversations, which really said nothing at all. No. The universe was pretty clear on this one. If Matt cared for me not even more than a friend but as a friend, if he loved me a little bit on a basic human level, he would be there with me, helping Evan do contortions in the tree tops and not, I repeat, NOT trying to get the cute bartender in pigtails to give him her phone number.

86

One Tiny Detail

Watching Matt flirt with the bartender (whom I didn't know and was just helping for the evening), I thought of several scenarios:

1) I could burst into tears and run to my mom and Megan (I have done this before.)

2) I could call him a mutha-fucker and take out a baseball bat and say "Time to rumble!" (I've wanted to do this before.)

3) Or I could ignore it. Store my energy for later.

I ignored it. I was not about to mess up my whole life by making a scene with a man who might have been the love of my life, or just a really bad two-year obsession. I was just now starting to think the second option sounded more likely. And then a strange thing happened. She didn't give him her number. I saw him lean in towards her, hand her his cell phone, and then . . . well, she shook her head, laughed and handed it back to him.

So instead of practicing an ancient castration rite with

a pair of rocks, I turned my back, took a deep breath and looked at the checklist. Lights, food, fortuneteller, obstacle course, music. Everything was going good except the music.

Holly fuckety! The music! I'd planned a fundraiser to raise money for the Grand Rapids Music Center and I'd forgotten to book music for the event! How was this possible? HOW?

Someone pulled on my shirtsleeve. "What do you think?" Evan asked, pointing to the trees. "I mean, you can't really tell right now but I'm fairly certain that I calculated it right and anyway, at night time those trees are going to light up like . . . You crying or something?"

"What?" I asked. I was still staring at the trees but all I could see were branches and leaves and everything was getting all blurry. Shit. I was crying. "I forgot about the music," I whispered.

"Oh." Evan said and we both stared up at the heavens hoping for a miracle.

87

One Tiny Miracle

Miracles, you know? They do happen. And they arrive in very unlikely packages. My miracle came in the form of a certain ex-fiancé's current lover, the small, compact, and very fierce Salomé . I'd had Amber and Salomé waiting in the wings for the big Reveal, hoping I would change my mind and maybe not do the thing I was planning on doing: ejecting Matt from my life. It turns out, Fate stepped in anyway. As soon as I realized my huge fuck up, I grasped Evan's hand and breathed, "Go. Now. Find someone. Anyone." He nodded and he was off. Five minutes later, Salomé stomped over and said, "I'm in a band. I'll call them. If you want." She looked up at Amber who nodded. "And you don't have to pay us or whatever. Consider us even for, you know, the whole barroom brawl thing."

I couldn't help myself. I stooped down and gave Salomé a big-ol-bear-hug.

And then before I knew it, the Kicking it Under the Stars event was on. Complete with a punk rock cover band composed of Little People.

88

One Moment To Breathe . . .

"Wow," Lisa said, looking around. "You're going to kill our board. They're going to have heart attacks when they see this!" She said this not like it was a bad thing, but like she was really excited.

I couldn't help myself. I was feeling excited too.

It was 6:30 and there were people there. A lot of people. Weird, wacky, wonderful people. At my event. And more cars kept coming. It was going to be a success! I could feel it in my bones. Now if only all those people brought cash with them to give away.

"Take a minute before things get crazy," Lisa said. "Look around, and enjoy. And then get cracking. We need sixteen thousand dollars in four hours."

I tried not to think on that, so I just took a deep breath and looked at my event. My event. The event I'd created. I felt a little bit like I'd given birth, without, you know, the giving birth part.

It was just starting to get dark out and everything was slipping into blue. In the treetops you could see the faint glimmer of what, in an hour or so, would be a galaxy of lights. I looked for Evan (who was serving Klingon Soup) and gave him the thumbs up. He really was adorable, in a dorky, endearing, platonic sort of way. And there was Julie (followed by little Janeway complete with Vulcan ears) and her team serving amazing food. The table actually smoked and was complete with a starship centerpiece that was, yes, 100% edible.

Bud, in his black leather outfit and handlebar mustache, stood ready at the bar, having sent his pig-tailed helper to sell serve cocktails. He looked wild and inviting at the same time and I think guests weren't quite sure whether he was serving drinks or giving S&M tips. My mom was there too, of course, swathed in layers of fabric, her green hair now a deep crimson (aided by extensions). She had a table set near the ropes course where for twenty dollars you could get your fortune told. I'd made her promise that she'd only give good fortunes but she just rolled her eyes and said "I'll call them as I read them, dear," which I knew meant that they'd be good fortunes unless someone pissed her off.

Megan was my Go To Woman. She was at my side waiting to run and do anything aiding with things like the following: Need more napkins? Hop to it, Chad. Need more ice? Go Amber. Need a backrub? That creepy woman in the scarves will probably help you out.

Megan was currently telling people where to park followed by Chad . . . who'd brought a collection of people with him down from the Island, people who no doubt 'owed him one'.

And underneath all of it, playing like a soundtrack, under every crazy mixed-up portion of this event was the steady (yet strangely alluring) sounds of the Mighty Small: Salomé's punk rock band that also preformed traditional Celtic music. They stood in a little clearing in the center, canopied by the star-lit leaves, giving them plenty of space to rock out. They might have been wee, but their sound was mighty.

And Matt? Where was Matt in all of this? It's funny. I spent so much time soaking in the event that I'd forgotten about my other purpose, my Mmm. There he was, standing at the Trust Fall, ready to talk paying customers to fall into his arms. Now that things were rolling, I wondered if I could finally do what I'd decided I wanted to do. And it wasn't fall into his arms.

"Chloe!" He called and smiled at me warmly. He waved. I waved. Megan said, "Go get him, Tiger," and I did.

89

One Sad Good-Bye

"Hey, there," he said and smiled at me. Matt's smile could liquefy steel. It just wasn't working on me tonight for some reason. "This is some event you planned, huh?" He gently pushed my shoulder in an 'aw, shucks' kind of way.

"Yeah, it's going pretty well." I took a deep breath. I was losing confidence fast. Then I saw one of Matt's other friends, a cute redhead standing by a tree. She looked at me and gave me the thumbs up. Then two other women, Beth and Rachel, beautiful blond sisters nodded their heads. They were sending me good juju. I wasn't just going to do this for me, I was doing this for all of his girlfriends who'd been misled into thinking there was something more. I took a deep breath and started again: "Look, I wanted to uhm . . ." awkward pause here while I tried to think of something to say, "I wanted to tell you something important." I wanted to tell him that maybe we were just friends, and I was realizing more and more that that was okay with me. In fact, I wasn't even sure I needed him as a friend so much since I had Megan and my mom and now, strangely, Amber and Evan and Chad and even Salomé. My life was getting pretty full and I was tired of wasting so much energy on him.

"I wanted to tell you something too," he said and then leaned in close to my ear. He still smelled good to me: musky, but I suddenly realized that the scent was more perfume than pheromone. His voice was low, but it didn't have an effect on me. Not even when he said these magic words: "I wanted to tell you that later tonight, if you want, we can finally do it. I know you've been waiting a long time so if you want . . . tonight's the night. I'm your man. Tonight." He looked at me and I got the gist of what he was also not-saying: that for tonight he'd be my man, but that didn't necessarily include tomorrow night. I wondered what would have happened if that woman had given him her phone number.

He kissed my cheek and then pulled back and winked at me. Actually, winked! Well, if that didn't convince me. A wink was about as sexy as . . . a lollipop or something. I felt like: Oh, goody! We could finally Do It. Yippee! (Note the heavy sarcasm here.)

Why wasn't I excited about this? Why? Because he was offering to have sex with me like it was some kind of favor, like I'd been asking him to make me a cheeseburger and he was finally willing to go through the trouble of lighting the BBQ. Where was the romance? Where was the passion? Where was the fire?

There wasn't any.

There wasn't any because the sad truth was, I was a stranger to Matt, and in some ways, in every way, he was a stranger to me. I'd built this fantasy up in my head that he was The One without really looking at who he was as a person. We had little in common, he didn't make me laugh, and our couch cuddle time had long slipped into boredom. And I think that maybe he did love me . . . as a person . . . as a friend. He genuinely cared for me. But it wasn't enough. Not by a long shot. What I said next came as a surprise to me: "Yeah, well, thanks for the offer there, buddy, but I'm afraid I'm going to pass. You're too late."

His face flushed crimson. "What do you mean I'm too late?" He looked at me and a flash of anger or something blipped across his face.

"You're just too late, Matt. I'm not . . . I don't think of you that way anymore." As soon as I said it, I realized it was true.

"Wait a minute!" he said, his voice rising. He reached for my arm. "You're like obsessed with me or something. You're Constant Chloe, always in the background. So I thought I'd finally toss you a bone. That's what you want, isn't it?"

Toss you a bone? TOSS ME A BONE? And wait a minute here, buckaroo, had he actually called me Constant Chloe? Is that how he referred to me when I wasn't with him? Not as the love of his life, but as Constant Chloe, which sort of felt like Constant Chlamydia?

I hate to tell you what I did next. I don't really have any justifiable defense for this action because it was more of a reaction to his huge blunder. I was not obsessed with him. He was not The One. I simply lifted my knee strategically into his groin, making him do one of those guttural 'ugh' sounds before falling onto the ground.

"Thanks for letting us use the Happy Place, Matt." I said. "We're even now. You don't owe me anything else."

I turned around and left him there, realizing as I turned away that Matt had made the biggest blunder of all: he'd underestimated me. At any rate, I had an event to run and my mom needed help organizing the line that was queuing up to talk to her. And even though the huge crowd that was gathering was cheering for the end of the Mighty Small's first set, I still felt like they were cheering for me. Maybe a few of them were.

90

The Let Down

Bad nights and great nights all end at some point, and this one was a little of both. After Matt started breathing again, he stood up, only to be kicked in the balls by thirty or so perfect women who'd had enough of being dicked around. Well, maybe they didn't all kick him in the balls, I'm speaking more poetically here, but the effect was the same: gone was Matt's bravado. In the end, he was just a lonely little boy.

But the event itself was a huge success. People walked the rope course illumined by the twinkling of stars and Christmas lights. They paid for fortunes from my mom and made donations for the amazing food. They paid twenty bucks to throw darts at a board and win stupid prizes. And when they were good and liquored up and their bellies were full and everyone was warm and happy, we all danced in the moonlight with the Mighty Small and Megan, at long last, told me she felt like a real honest-to-goodness elf.

And then it was over. We picked up the plates and napkins, the leftover glasses of wine, the empty beer bottles. Stacked the tables, unstrung the lights, pulled down the signs, hugged, said our goodbyes, and then, we drove away.

I didn't have another conversation with Matt. I'd like to think he watched us go. I'd like to think that he was a little bit sad to see me leave not only the Happy Place, but also his life, because that was what I was doing. Something in me shifted that night, and it wasn't going to shift back. As sad as that sounds, it was actually a very good thing.

91

The Verdict

"Christ, Buddha, and Jumpin' Jehoshaphat," I said. "I can't look at the total. Can you just tell me if I have a job tomorrow or not?" I was in Lisa's office two days after the event. She'd called me in to 'settle accounts'. I was terrified this involved her giving me a check and telling me never to contact her again.

"Do you have a job tomorrow?" repeated Lisa. God, my stomach was doing nosedives. I hoped I wasn't developing a sudden case of diarrhea. Really, that couldn't come at a worse time, and I'd come to learn that my body was against me. My stomach rumbled. "You do have a job tomorrow. And the day after that and after that . . . and well, I'd like to invite you onboard."

Invite me onboard? WTF? I opened my eyes and looked behind me, just, you know, to be sure I was the only one in the room. "You mean we did it? We made sixteen thousand dollars? The event worked?" I didn't mean to sound mystified, but I was. It was the craziest event I'd ever been to, and I was the one who planned it. I could only imagine what the board members were saying.

"We did not make sixteen thousand dollars," she said soberly, then quickly followed it with: "We made *sixty* thousand dollars. Sixty! Fucking! Thousand!" She screamed. I screamed. We jumped up and clung to each other like soap opera stars at a funeral . . . only this . . . this was a celebration. Holy moly. I couldn't believe it! I'd done it! I'd done something that wasn't a fuck up!

But I still didn't understand. After I got my body functions under control, Lisa sat me down and explained. We made several thousand on the ticket sales, and then there were donations for the band, for the food, silent auction items, the fortuneteller, the dart board, and when people started drinking, money started flowing. On those things alone we made nearly twenty thousand dollars, but what put us over the top was a very special donation made by one Mr. Boyle, aged eighty-seven and he wanted to thank me especially for bringing my mother to help him improve his life. "Oh god, tell me she didn't . . ." I began.

Lisa nodded. "Your mother apparently gave Mr. Boyle some tantric sex secrets, and this morning he waltzed in here, handed me a check and told me he and Mrs. Boyle had never been happier."

I sat back in my chair. Leave it to my mom.

Suddenly my spirit dropped. I didn't really deserve the job; it was more of my mom's doing and not mine. I started to say that to Lisa but she stopped me.

"You know what I like about you Chloe?" She looked at me. I shrugged my shoulders. I honestly didn't know why anyone liked me. "I like you because you're interesting. You're a collector. A collector of experiences and people. Strange things come your way and if the rest of us out there, the boring people, if we're lucky enough, we get sucked up in your life for one night. Kicking It Under the Stars was like that, was like being sucked in to the chaos. And yes, your mom helped get the donation, but she, dear girl, was there because of you. And only you."

I think I cried then. I really did. And then I floated all the way home.

I sort of liked thinking of myself as Chloe Knaggs, Collector of People than Chloe Knaggs, Blunder Woman, though I think the blunder part will always be a little bit of who I am too.

92

What Happens Next . . .

There was only one thing left to do: celebrate. I called an impromptu party at my apartment and by the time I got there, it was already heating up. Megan swooped me up in her arms as soon as I walked in the door. "A job! A job! A job!" she chanted. "I know," I said. "It's a miracle."

"Phooey on miracles," Mom said, pulling me to her bosom (which was covered in a teal sweatshirt decorated like a peacock feather). "There's no such thing as a miracle. You brought this on yourself. This is fate."

I didn't want to discuss the difference between miracle and fate (was there one?) so I just hugged Mom back.

Evan was next. He handed me a beer and extended his hand. "We have two hundred and eighty six days until we consummate our relationship, Chloe. I think a handshake is an appropriate first step." I gave him an awkward hug instead.

"Listen, Evan," I said. "I need to talk to you about the whole 'consummating' thing. I'm just not sure . . ." An image of Matt flashed in front of my mind and how he'd kept me hanging on by holding conversations with me that weren't clear. If he had said from the beginning 'we are only friends' would I have wasted so much time and energy and love on him? I needed to be honest with Evan. "Evan, I don't think you and I are ever going to be more than just friends. I don't want you hanging on for something else. In fact, right now, I don't want to be more than friends with anyone."

"So that means in two hundred and eighty six days . . ." He looked at me questioningly.

"Maybe we'll just go see a movie instead."

He paused. Took out his little notebook, scratched something out, and scribbled something instead. "That's okay with me, Chloe. I'm not very good in the relationship department. But I would certainly enjoy a movie. And maybe . . ." Don't say it Evan don't say it! "Some chicken wings and beer." He smiled. I loved him just a little bit then.

I sat on the couch surrounded by Megan and Chad, my mom, Evan, and later Amber and Salomé, Julie and Bud, and some of the girls from Matt's collection. We drank beer, watched "Picnic" and "Valley of the Dolls" and ordered Chinese, Indian, Ethiopian, and pizza. It was the perfect night.

And what would happen with me and Matt? Nothing. Not a thing. I looked at Chad and Megan, how they sat next to each other, his hand on her thigh, how comfortable they seemed and I realized that what I wanted wasn't drama. I didn't want to work so hard at making love work. It should just happen. It should be as effortless as this party.

I smiled, knowing there was a crinkled little note in my

pocket telling me that someone wanted to whisk me away somewhere. I no longer cared who penned it. All that mattered was that there was someone out there who was going to be crazy about me. I just needed to find them. And you know . . . it could wait.

I leaned back. "A little Reiki, darling?" Mom offered, thinking maybe I needed some extra healing.

"No, Mom," I said. "You know, right now, I'm doing just fine."

THE END

About The Author

Tanya Eby is a novelist and narrator and lives in Michigan with her tiki-obsessed husband and two quirky kiddos. Find out more about her work and her life by visiting her website tanyaeby.com.

You can also find her on Twitter at @Blunder_Woman and on Facebook at facebook.com/TanyaEbyWriter.